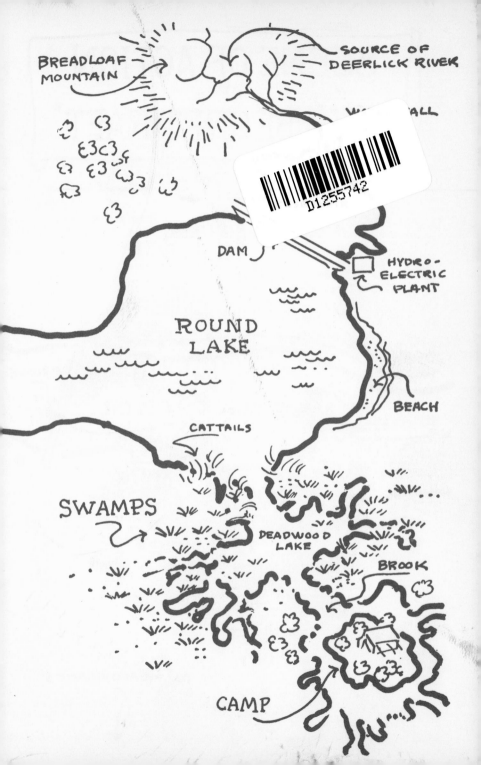

The Secret Raft

WEEKLY READER
CHILDREN'S BOOK CLUB

THE VANGUARD PRESS, INC. *New York*

WEEKLY READER CHILDREN'S BOOK CLUB

presents

THE SECRET RAFT

by *Hazel Krantz*

Author of "100 Pounds of Popcorn"

ILLUSTRATED BY CHARLES GEER

Copyright, © 1965, by Hazel Krantz
Published simultaneously in Canada by the
Copp Clark Publishing Company, Ltd., Toronto
*No portion of this book may be reproduced in any
form without the written permission of the publisher,
except by a reviewer who may wish to quote brief
passages in connection with a review for a newspaper
or magazine.*
Library of Congress Catalogue Card Number: 65-17372

Weekly Reader Book Club Edition

Contents

The Secret Raft

1: The Strange Men

On the Monday of the spring vacation Howie Blake had a very funny dream. He thought he was down at the main switchboard of the Telephone Company and all the phones were ringing at once. He tried pulling out all the plugs but the telephones kept ringing right in his ear.

Howie opened one eye. It was still dark except for the light of the street lamp streaming through the window. The ringing kept on next to his ear. He opened his other eye and turned his head on the pillow. There was something knobby under the pillow right where the ringing was coming from.

Then he remembered. He had planned to go down to the Deerlick River with his friend Joel Matson and Joel's twin sister, Diane, and watch the sun come up. He'd placed an alarm clock set for five o'clock under his pillow so he'd be sure to get up in time. That was where the ringing was coming from.

Hastily, he reached under the pillow and took out the clock, shutting it off before it woke the whole family. His sixteen-year-old brother Paul in the next bed rolled over and muttered "Arumph." Howie watched him nervously until he was sure Paul had fallen back asleep. It wasn't that he was trying to keep things from Paul, but this idea of getting up early to see the sunrise was a private thing, just for himself and the Matson twins.

He groped his way out of bed and padded over to where he had laid out his clothes the night before. Nestled comfortably on top of his chino pants was a black ball of fur. As Howie approached, the ball unwound itself and a black and brown beagle head lifted itself up to look at him in shocked surprise.

"Off, Pepper," Howie ordered the dog, tilting the chair to help him along.

Pepper resentfully slid off the chair with a small growl, then stretched and yawned and immediately forgave Howie for interrupting his sleep. He wagged his tail, then scampered over to the door and started scratching on it.

"Quiet, boy," Howie warned. "You'll spoil everything."

Pepper stopped scratching and waited patiently while Howie slipped into his clothes. Howie tiptoed past Paul's bed, opened the bedroom door quietly, and, with Pepper at his heels, scurried past the rooms where his parents and little sister Cindy were sleeping.

He ran down to the kitchen and started gathering supplies for a breakfast picnic. Reaching up to the shelf on which his mother kept paper supplies, he tried to take one paper bag. A whole bunch of paper bags, a paper towel roll, and a box of aluminum foil slid off the shelf and onto the floor.

His glance traveled from the jumble on the floor to the window. He could see a rim of light beginning to appear in the sky to the east. He had to hurry, or he'd miss the sunrise. There was no time to pick things up.

Leaving the stuff strewn across the floor, he opened the refrigerator and started stuffing food into the bag. He took a box of eggs, some butter, a loaf of bread, and a big hunk of cake.

He ran over to the back door and opened it, Pepper whisking out ahead of him. Howie started to follow the dog, but then he remembered you can't cook eggs without a frying pan. He rushed over to the pot cabinet and hauled out pots until he came to the frying pan. He was about to put the pots back into the cabinet when he heard Pepper barking outside. That was all he needed . . . a big racket from Pepper!

Casting one guilty look at the kitchen floor, full of pots and paper towels and bags, he grabbed his frying pan and food supplies and ran out the door. He whistled Pepper away from a tree where the dog was expecting a squirrel to come down and fight, and started down the hill toward the Matsons' house.

As Pepper circled around him searching out interesting early-morning smells, Howie felt very glad the dog was along. Sometimes he imagined Pepper was the only one who really thought much of him. It wasn't that his family wasn't nice to him—his parents were kind, his big brother didn't treat him too much like a kid, even though Paul was four years older, and his five-year-old sister was cute, although a bit of a nuisance. It was just that while Paul and Cindy kept on bringing their parents pleasure, Howie seemed to produce just aggravation.

Walking down the hill in the somber gray of predawn, he thought sad thoughts. He remembered with pain a day just before vacation. It was a busy day for his parents, all right. In the morning they had to get to the high school, where Paul was being inducted into the National Honor Society. His mother had been telling all the relatives about it on the telephone.

She didn't mention the afternoon's activities to the relatives. That was when she had the conference with Mr. Frost, Howie's sixth-grade teacher, about how Howie was failing English. On the way out of the school, Mr. Dunham, the principal, called her into his office to discuss the matter of a fight Howie had had with Ralph Murphy in the school cafeteria.

Later, when Howie and his mother were sitting down in the kitchen for a deadly quiet talk about having his English homework signed by his parents and the no-television, no-movies, no-baseball punishment for the Ralph Murphy fight, Cindy had come bursting into the house waving a note in her pudgy little hand.

After reading the note, Mrs. Blake had gone into a dither again, just as she had when she learned about Paul and the Honor Society. It seemed that Cindy had been selected to play the fairy queen in the kindergarten spring play! His mother had turned to Howie and had said hastily, "Now, remember everything we've talked about. I don't want to go through this with you again." Then she took Cindy by the hand and rushed off to the store to buy pink material for a costume.

Howie should have been grateful for the interruption, but he wasn't. He wandered about the house feeling kind of flat and thinking of all the things he had wanted to tell his mother.

There wasn't much to say about the English except that he had gotten so interested in working on an experiment with his chemistry set, testing for starches in foods, he completely forgot to do his book report. His mother, he knew, wouldn't buy that excuse. But she might have understood about the Ralph Murphy thing.

All anyone knew was that he had socked Ralph, right in the middle of the school lunchroom. But no one had asked why.

Ralph had been bothering Howie for a long time, especially at lunchtime. He had a way of coming to lunch late and, when the duty teacher wasn't looking, worming his way in ahead of Howie on the line. Then, when Howie objected, he'd put on a sweet little innocent act and Howie would be scolded for creating a disturbance on the line.

On the day of the fight, Ralph went a little too far. As they were walking to their table carrying trays, he'd deliberately bumped into Howie. Down went Howie's tray, dishes clattering and food spilling. The whole lunchroom looked up and some little second-graders sitting at a nearby table started to snicker.

When Howie finally cleaned up the mess and came to the table with a new tray of food, Ralph started pointing at him and haw-hawing. Then Howie lost his temper and gave Ralph a good punch. Ralph let out a yell as if he were being attacked by lions.

Sweet little Mrs. Fisher, a first-grade teacher who was on duty at the time, ran over and separated the boys.

As he was being led away to the principal's office, Howie noticed how disturbed Mrs. Fisher looked and that made him feel worse than anything. Next to their own Mr. Frost, Mrs. Fisher was the teacher the sixth-graders liked best. She always admired the girls' hair-do's and remarked on pretty dresses. When she needed help in carrying a projector or putting away heavy things, she always said to Mr. Frost, "May I borrow one of your powerful big boys?"

Howie was often the one chosen. Although he wasn't the heaviest boy, he was certainly the tallest, and very good at reaching high places. After he did a job for Mrs. Fisher, she was so grateful he really did feel powerful.

After the fight, Mr. Dunham made him sit in the office while the other boys and girls went out to the playground after lunch. All the time he was sitting there, Howie kept thinking about how he got into such messes. If he'd stopped to think, he wouldn't have caused trouble either for himself or for Mrs. Fisher. Ralph Murphy needed a lesson, it was true, but Howie didn't have to hit him in the lunchroom. He could have taken care of him on the way home from school.

If only he'd thought first before he hit!

As he walked down the street toward the Matsons' house, he felt a little angry, not at anybody special, but because trouble always seemed to find him. He felt like throwing something, so he picked up a stick, threw it, and said to Pepper, "Fetch."

The dog obediently wagged his pointed tail and brought back the stick. He laid it at Howie's feet and looked up at him with moist brown eyes. Howie knelt down and scratched Pepper behind the ears, just a little too hard. The dog whimpered slightly and Howie rubbed the place where he had hurt him, saying, "I'm sorry. I'm sorry." The little dog wagged his tail very hard, as if to say, "I know you didn't mean it."

Howie stood up again and started running very fast toward the Matsons' house. He jumped over the Matsons' hedge and dropped the bad thoughts behind him. Very quietly he stole up to Joel's bedroom window. The Matsons had a ranch house, so Howie was able to knock softly on the window.

Joel's head popped up.

"Hurry," said Howie in a stage whisper.

Joel nodded and disappeared. After a few minutes, he and his sister Diane came out the back door, each carrying a bulging paper bag.

Whenever Howie saw them, he always marveled that the two were twins. They didn't even look enough alike to be brother and sister. Joel had red hair that always seemed to stick out in front of his head like a shelf, no matter how he combed it. He was bony thin and about six inches shorter than Howie, which didn't mean he was short. Everyone his own age was shorter than Howie.

Diane was built like Joel, with skinny arms and legs, but she was very dark, almost like an Indian. She had black hair, very soft and straight, that always seemed to be flying in every direction. Diane's eyes, however, were what you noticed most about her. They were dark brown and always seemed to be excited or angry or unhappy. Howie didn't think he'd ever seen Diane's eyes look just plain calm.

Right now they were excited, as the three raced through Callahan's apple orchard toward the river.

"Come on! Come on!" she urged. "We don't want to miss it."

She ran ahead, her red sweater flapping like a banner. The boys raced after her, laughing, and Pepper kept running among the three of them in figure eights. The world around them was still and gray, waiting for the dawn, and the three felt that for this space of time, when everyone else was sleeping, the earth was theirs alone.

They scrambled down a grassy slope on the bank of the Deerlick and flopped down, panting, in the shelter of a little grove of willows.

There was the dank smell of the water and a moist greeny fragrance of spring things growing. A mist hung over the river like a magic curtain. It rose slowly and dreamily over the flat gray water and disappeared in wisps into the sky.

The water lay revealed in a leaden stillness, but soon a light started to spread over the tops of the dark hills across the river.

"I can almost hear trumpets sounding 'Here comes the sun,'" murmured Diane.

The boys smiled. Diane was always saying funny things like that. But she was right. The slivers of light coming up from behind the hills were heralds of the real thing, for now the sun itself came riding up above the hills, bathing everything in a sudden radiance.

All the hazy look of dawn disappeared and objects on the other side of the river stood out hard and sharp. There were the houses of the town of Sumner, and farther up the river, Sumner's factories and piers and the bridge linking Sumner with their own village of Thorneywoods.

Far to the north of Sumner rose the wooded hulk of Breadloaf Mountain, where the Deerlick had its source. You could see the narrow trickle of the river coming down the mountain until it tumbled down Princess Falls into a bed of foam.

An earthen dam had been constructed to catch the hurrying water and let it down, through a system of pipes, nice and easy, into the small Round Lake before it started its journey to the ocean.

Howie could just see the big white hydroelectric plant that transformed the wild energy of the river into power for the whole area.

The swamplands were nearby, extending mysteriously beyond Round Lake. There were all sorts of wild legends about the swamplands, which had been formed during a long-ago flood. Some people said it was a hideout for criminals, especially one invented by older children to frighten small children, Murderer One-Eye. But everyone granted that the swamplands were dangerous and unhealthy and that something should be done about it.

Howie's own feeling about the swamplands was a kind of scared excitement. He'd never been beyond the outer edge, where he went to gather cattails. But every time he thought about them he felt as if a magnet were drawing him there. Someday he was going to explore the swamplands.

His eyes wandered along the bank on his own side of the river. There were the small docks of Thorneywoods, used mostly for pleasure boats, the ramshackle boathouse, the ancient shoe factory that dated back to mill wheel days, and a cluster of new electronics plants where Howie's father worked as an engineer.

"You know," said Howie lazily, "I think I'd rather live in Sumner than Thorneywoods."

"Why would you want to live there?" asked Joel in surprise. "It's a big town full of noise. And the streets are all hills."

Howie's eyes narrowed. "Just look at the location of Sumner and the location of Thorneywoods," he argued. "If the dam ever broke, Sumner would be safe, but what would happen to Thorneywoods? It would be flooded in no time."

Diane's eyes darkened and grew wide. "A flood! We'd all have to sit on the tops of our houses!"

The three gazed at the placid river, now silver in the sunlight. An early tugboat tooted its way up the river, drawing a barge full of lumber. It seemed impossible that this tame river could ever cause trouble, but they knew its history.

Before the dam had been built, twenty-five years before, no one could live on the Thorneywoods side of the river because of the rampaging floods that spread over the land each spring. The only building there was the shoe factory, and that was built on stilts.

But the dam had changed all that. First, farmers like

Howie's grandfather had come to work the land, now known as Meadowland, where the river had deposited rich silt during the annual floods. Grandfather Blake still had his prosperous apple orchard over in Meadowland.

Then people who were not farmers started to settle on the Thorneywoods side, away from the smoke and grime of Sumner. Thorneywoods had grown into a attractive little suburb. But the people who lived there knew that the safety of their pleasant houses and neat lawns depended on one thing—the dam that kept the Deerlick from flooding.

"This is silly," said Joel sensibly. "The dam is not going to break; it's much too strong. Come on, let's eat. My stomach is rubbing up against my backbone."

They stood up and flapped their arms to get warm. The spring sunshine still had an edge of chill in it.

"If you take the stuff out of the bags," Howie suggested to Diane, "Joel and I will gather some firewood."

As Howie and Joel headed toward the woods they heard Diane call, "Hey, Joel, I thought you brought a bag with bacon in it."

"Never can find anything," Joel grumbled. The boys turned around and went back to Diane.

"It was right here. Small brown bag. There were knives and forks in it too," said Joel.

"Where?" demanded Diane.

Then Howie noticed that Pepper was missing. He glanced at the beach. "Uh, uh," he said. There was the dog, charging along with a brown paper bag in his mouth.

"Pepper, bring that back!" yelled Howie, chasing him.

Pepper paused in flight long enough to give Howie a guilty look, then ducked his head and ran away, the paper bag going bumpity-bump along the beach.

Pepper stopped, took another look at Howie, and ran on. The bag ripped, and knives, forks, and bacon soon scattered all over the sand.

Howie stopped chasing the dog and started picking up the things from the ground. Pepper scurried into the bushes with the paper bag still clenched in his teeth.

Joel and Diane started to laugh when Howie came up to them, pieces of bacon dangling from his hands, muttering, "That miserable little beast. Can't trust him for a moment! I brought back the silver, too. Better not lose that!"

Diane took the sandy bacon and looked it over. "Don't worry," she said. "I'll just wash it off and it'll be as good as new."

Howie and Joel went back to the woods and managed to find some dry firewood and twigs. They brought it back and made a ring of stones to hold the fire. Then they piled some paper napkins in the center of the ring and built a little tent out of the twigs on top of the paper.

After using half a pack of matches and burning his fingers, Howie finally got the napkins to burn long enough to ignite the twigs. Then the boys started putting on the bigger pieces of wood, slowly and carefully so they wouldn't smother the fire. The flames spread their fingers along the dry wood and soon the lovely smell of wood smoke began to mix with the tang of the

sharp spring air. The three crouched before the fire until the leaping flames died down a little. It was lovely and warm.

Diane spread out the bacon on the frying pan and Joel went to get more wood.

"Let me fry the bacon," Howie suggested. "I know just how to do it."

Diane handed over the frying pan and stuck a piece of bread on a barbecue fork. "Only way to get real toast," she said, holding it over the fire.

"You bet," Howie replied.

"It sure is smoky," coughed Diane, backing away a little.

Howie didn't answer. He was having his own troubles. First he tried to bend over the fire with the frying pan, but he found the flames nearly singeing his hair, so he lay prone and stuck the pan into the fire that way. Then he smelled something burning and noticed that the handle of the pan was glowing. Little bits of charred wood dropped off the handle. He put the pan back into the fire just a little way, keeping the handle clear.

Diane dropped a scorched piece of toast onto a paper plate and speared another piece of bread on her fork. "Why can't we just eat bread and butter?" she complained, wiping her smarting eyes.

"Don't be a quitter," scolded Howie. "A little smoke won't hurt you."

Diane set her lips and shoved the fork back into the fire, closing her eyes against the smoke. If there was one thing she could not stand, it was being called a quitter.

Joel reappeared with more wood. "Something smells great!" he exclaimed. "How's the bacon?"

"Almost done," Howie replied. "We can fry the eggs in the bacon fat."

The bacon was sizzling in nice little bubbles. Joel put down the wood and took over the toast-making, while Diane unpacked paper plates.

"Just a tiny bit more," sang out Howie. "Then we'll be ready for those eggs." He smiled with contentment in spite of the fact that his arm was getting tired and his face was too hot for comfort.

Then he heard a pop and something hot landed on his wrist. "Yeeow!" he shouted, and dropped the frying pan. Pieces of bacon leaped into the fire and curled up into black little splinters.

Howie jumped up and down holding on to his wrist. "Hot fat fell on my wrist," he howled.

Diane grabbed hold of him as he danced past and smeared butter on the burn. The stinging stopped, but Howie looked mournfully at the bacon disappearing into the fire. "All that work for nothing," he said.

"At least we can have fried eggs," said Joel.

Diane reached for the pan. "I'll do the frying," she said firmly. With expert twists of the wrist she jerked the pan in and out of the fire until the eggs formed neat brownish rings in the pan.

As they sat eating the eggs and toast, a bird overhead sent a sharp trill into the air. Howie whistled back, trying to imitate the notes.

Pepper thought it was a dog whistle and came bounding out of the bushes where he had been hiding in shame. He stood next to Howie and wagged his tail expectantly.

Howie looked at him severely. "Bad dog," he scolded. "Why did you run away with our things?"

At the unfriendly sound of Howie's voice, the tail stopped wagging. Sadly, Pepper turned around and lay down. But he was right back again when Diane started putting eggs onto Howie's plate. He looked at the food mournfully.

Howie took a forkful. The eggs were a little underdone, but they had a certain delicious taste you didn't get at home.

Pepper barked plaintively.

"Oh, all right," Howie sighed. "You are a terrible dog, but I can't let you starve."

He threw Pepper a piece of egg white. Then he gave him some of the burned toast. Pepper gobbled up the food, then came over and snuggled against Howie. Howie scratched him behind the ears to show he was forgiven and Pepper put his face in his master's lap and snuffled contentedly.

But as soon as Diane started frying more eggs, Pepper turned toward her with his old suffering expression. Finally she had to make an egg just for him on his own paper plate.

They finished eating and tossed their plates into the fire. It flared for a moment, then settled down to a low crackle. The three sat cross-legged around it, watching the awakening life of the river.

More boats had followed the first barge—an excursion steamer starting a sight-seeing trip down the river, small freighters, and an occasional motorboat. A train chugged along on the opposite shore and plumes of smoke arose from the factories. The bridge between Sumner and Thorneywoods was alive with cars, looking like little colored bugs, shooting across it in both directions.

The fire died down to ashy embers. They started to feel chilly.

"Let's go for a walk," said Diane, jumping up.

The boys stood up, stretched their muscles, and then threw dirt on the fire until they were sure it was out. Diane gathered up the frying pan and silverware and washed them, more or less, at the river.

"Let's go down under the piers and holler," suggested Joel.

With Pepper running in circles around them, they headed for the rickety old piers. Right now they stretched out over the stony beach into the river, still streaked by the winter rains and completely deserted. But soon they would be the center of interest for the people of Thorneywoods and their pleasure boats.

The three ran some races along the piers, then went underneath to poke around the old blackened posts and to try out the echo.

"Whoo-ooo," called Howie. "I'm the ghost of the pirate Redbeard. If you find my treasure, you will be cursed by the skull and crossbones!"

"Whoo-ooo," the echo came back. Then they heard another noise that wasn't an echo. It was the sound of footsteps on the pier overhead.

Joel clutched Howie in mock horror. "There goes Redbeard making the fair maiden walk the plank."

Howie squinted through a crack in the pier floor to

see who was tramping around. At first he could see only some heavy shoes. Then his eye traveled up and he viewed three men whom he had never noticed around Thorneywoods. Two of the men were very young and the third had gray hair. They were dressed in rough-looking jackets like fishermen.

They had boxes of canned food, a couple of suitcases, and what looked like a folded-up tent. Apparently, they were going camping.

But it wasn't the camping equipment that interested Howie. It was the other things they were carrying. First of all, they had a radio and a transmitter. He could see that. Then there was a round thing all covered with canvas. Maybe that was the generator for the radio.

Queerest of all were a number of small packages, all thickly wrapped. The gray-haired man was being very fussy about those.

"Hey," whispered Howie to Joel and Diane. "Look."

They put their eyes to the crack.

"What do you think?" asked Howie.

"I don't know," said Joel slowly. "Those men are new around here. Looks fishy to me."

Diane turned around, her brown eyes shining with excitement. "Spies!" she exclaimed. "That's what they are!"

Howie took another look. "Do you really think so?"

"Sure," Diane continued. "Why else would they want a radio? They want to relay secrets to their government."

"Aw," mocked Joel, "you always let your imagination run away with you. They're probably only fishermen."

Diane looked at him in disgust. "Silly," she said. "What would fishermen be doing with bombs?"

"What bombs?" asked Howie, craning his neck to see better.

"Look!" Diane pointed to the thickly wrapped packages. "What else could they be? Bombs. The spies will get the order over the radio from their government telling them when to blow up the hydroelectric plant."

"How did you figure that out?" Joel scoffed.

"It's simple," Diane insisted. "The hydroelectric plant is the only thing around here an enemy would be interested in. Think of it—with the electricity knocked out, all the power in this whole valley would be gone!"

"You've been seeing too many television programs," her brother laughed. But he raised himself on his toes to see better.

"Stay down," hissed Howie. "Do you want them to see us?"

The men were loading a rather shabby-looking motorboat with the supplies.

"You'd think with all the money their government spends on spies, they'd buy a better boat," snorted Joel.

"Don't be dumb," said Howie. "They don't want people to notice them."

Just then Pepper noticed a school of little fish darting through the shallows. He splashed after them and, when the fish swam out of his reach, started yipping with disappointment. Howie grabbed hold of him and put his hand over his muzzle to silence him. Meanwhile, he heard the sound of a motor starting.

"Watch where they're going," he whispered.

Diane and Joel ran and hid behind one of the pilings while Howie held on to the slippery dog. The motor of the boat coughed, then settled into a steady drone. Howie heard the splash of the boat through the water, then a diminishing roar as it made its way upriver.

Diane was jumping up and down saying, "I told you! I told you!"

Howie let go of Pepper and ran over to Joel and Diane.

"See," she shouted. "They're heading for the swamplands. That's sort of near the hydroelectric plant."

Joel was becoming excited too now. He pushed his sister back behind the piling. "Do you want them to see you?" he asked.

The boat disappeared around the bend.

"They're going to the swamplands, all right," said Howie. "That's no place for honest campers. It's full of bogs and winding brooks."

"That's exactly why they're going to the swamps," said Joel, now thoroughly convinced. "It's their hide-out. They wouldn't pick a place where the whole world can see them."

Diane turned around dramatically. "Spies in our own town! And we're the only ones who know about them!"

"We have to tell the FBI," declared Joel.

"Wait," said Howie. "That might not be the right move. If the men are not spies, they can sue us for false arrest or something. We have to get the evidence first."

"How are we going to do that?" asked Diane.

"We'll follow them," Howie stated decisively.

"Oh, sure," said Joel. "We'll follow them. How? None

of us has a boat. What do you want to do, swim to the swamplands?"

Howie sat down and considered the problem. He looked around at the woods. "I know," he said, snapping his fingers. "We'll build a raft. There's plenty of wood around here. All we have to do is to cut it down."

2: Big Brother, Little Sister

Howie, Joel, and Diane crept out from under the pier and went into the woods to look for material suitable for a raft. There were plenty of trees with nice round limbs that could be cut into logs.

"Let's go home and get some saws," said Howie enthusiastically.

"I just thought of something," said Joel. "If people see us making a raft, won't they ask us why?"

"I never thought of that," admitted Howie.

"Well, then," continued Joel, "I think the first thing we have to do is to find a place to hide the raft."

They searched along the river bank for some kind of hidden shelter, like a cave. But there was no spot that was not right out in the open.

"Say," said Diane, "I remember a neat place. There's an old shack back in the woods. Come on."

She went thrashing through the bushes, ignoring the path. The boys followed.

"See," Diane shouted. "Isn't it beautiful?"

The boys emerged from the bushes to see Diane standing in a small clearing next to a tumbledown fisherman's shack.

Joel laughed. "Boy, you sure have some idea of beauty!"

"Look," said Diane, sounding like a real estate saleslady. "It's got a perfect hideaway underneath, just right for a raft."

The shack stood on stilts. The place beneath the stilts was dark and hidden by tall grasses. It was perfect for hiding a raft.

The boys eagerly crawled into the space under the shack. It was dim and spooky. The ground was sticky mud and full of dank wet trash.

"Whew," said Diane. "This place needs a house cleaning!"

Howie ran his hands over the muddy ground. "It's this wet ground I'm worried about. It can get the bottom of the raft all mildewed."

"We could bring some cardboard and lay it on the ground," suggested Joel.

"That's a good idea," nodded Howie. "We can get some cardboard boxes from the supermarket. Carton cardboard is strong."

"Meanwhile, let's get this junk out of here," said Diane, gathering up old tin cans and moldy rags.

The job of cleaning up turned out to be bigger than

they had expected. It looked as if fishermen had dumped their trash under the shack for years and years. They unearthed wet leaves, old newspapers, magazines, fish hooks, cans, empty match covers, rags, rusty nails, and bottles.

In order to hide the fact that someone was using the shack, they hauled the trash away bit by bit and piled it back in the woods. Then, when the crawl space was finally empty, they broke off tree branches and used them for brooms, sweeping the ground and knocking down the cobwebs.

"There, that's better," sighed Diane as she plopped down on the ground and rested her back against one of the stilts.

The boys sat down next to her, exhausted.

"It's too late to make a raft today," said Howie. "Let's do it tomorrow."

It was dim and scary under the shack, the kind of feeling that makes you think of ghost stories.

"I wonder if we'll see Murderer One-Eye out in the swamps," Diane shivered.

"There is no Murderer One-Eye," said her brother patiently. "That's just a made-up person children tell about."

"Could be thieves and murderers out there, though," Howie put in. "No one ever goes to the swamps. If I was a murderer, that's where I'd hide."

"I wouldn't want to be those spies," said Diane. "Can

you imagine camping out in a place full of desperate criminals?"

"Spies *are* desperate criminals," Howie reminded her. "No one is more desperate than a spy. They'll do anything."

"Oooh," said Diane. "Maybe we shouldn't go looking for them. . . . Can't we just tell the police?"

Howie looked at her sympathetically. "You don't have to go if you're afraid, Diane. This is no job for girls anyhow."

"I'm not afraid," Diane insisted quickly. "I'm not afraid of anything."

Joel picked up a stick and tried to balance it on one finger. "Howie," he said slowly, "do you really think this is such a good idea? I mean, those swamps are dangerous. We could get lost. I don't think our parents would like our going there."

Howie shrugged. "You don't have to tell your parents you're going. If they don't know about it, they can't forbid you to go. Then, when we capture the spies, we'll be heroes, and nobody gets mad at heroes. Unless," he looked Joel straight in the eye, "you would rather let the spies go ahead and blow up the hydroelectric plant just because you're scared of a little old swamp."

"Oh, no, of course not," said Joel, somewhat confused.

"All right, then," said Howie. "Tomorrow morning we'll meet at the supermarket and pick up the cardboard boxes for the ground. We have to bring saws to cut the logs, too."

"We need some rope to tie the logs together," Diane reminded him.

"That's right," said Howie. "We ought to bring ham-mers and nails, too."

They crawled out and stood in front of the shack, moving their arms in circles, trying to get the cricks out of their backs. Looking at the sun, they saw it was already mid-afternoon.

Howie followed the twins slowly, feeling happy right down to his fingertips at the thought of making the raft. He had to admit that he really didn't believe the men were spies—it was the thought of adventure that made him glow all over, the adventure of going to the swamps and finding out once and for all what secrets lay inside those winding streams.

After leaving Joel and Diane at their house, he ran up the hill, with Pepper racing on ahead. He swung open the back door and sniffed. Paul must be home. That would be the only reason for the smell of frying ham-burgers during the afternoon. Pepper smelled it too. He rushed ahead of Howie and stationed himself next to Paul, who sat in front of a plate of four hamburgers and a giant glass of milk reading *The Official Drivers' Test Handbook*. Paul was going for his learner's permit that week and was determined to memorize every word in the handbook so he would be sure not to fail the written test.

Paul was built big, like Howie, and looked more like eighteen than sixteen. But instead of straight brown hair and brown eyes, which Howie had inherited from their father, Paul had their mother's blue eyes and blond curly hair. When he was younger he used to wear his hair high on top of his head, but recently he'd started having it cut very short so only crisp little half curls showed. Their mother, who had always complained that Paul wouldn't have his hair cut, now sighed that he insisted on looking like a college man although he was only a junior in high school.

Pepper started crying piteously, eying every bite Paul took. At last Paul held up a piece of hamburger. Pepper sat up and begged. The piece of meat sailed through the air and the dog expertly snagged it.

"That's why he has such bad manners," said Howie, clomping the dirty frying pan into the kitchen sink. "Mother said not to feed him from the table."

"What can I do when he acts as if he's been lost on a desert for a month?" shrugged Paul. "So that's where it was."

"Where what was?" asked Howie.

"The big frying pan," said Paul. "I was looking all over for it."

Howie took a piece of steel wool and tried to clean off the sticky pan. The bacon grease just stayed there, mixed with sand.

"Here, Goofy, let me help you," said Paul after watching him struggle for a while. He reached under the sink and took out a bottle of grease remover and dumped some into the pan. Then he ran water on top of the grease remover. The bacon grease gently floated away.

Howie gratefully backed away from the sink and let his big brother clean the pan.

"Where have you been?" asked Paul.

"Oh, out with Joel and Diane."

"Down by the river?" Paul guessed.

"Yes. We wanted to watch the sun rise."

Paul grinned. "Did you?"

"Uh huh," said Howie briefly, not wanting to go into any further details. Looking in the package of frozen hamburgers, he came up with just one. "Boy, you sure leave a lot for other people."

Paul put the now clean frying pan on the stove. "Sorry," he said. "If I'd known you were coming, I'd have baked a cake. How about some eggs with that one hamburger?"

"I just had eggs," Howie sighed. "But okay, go back and eat your food. I can make them."

He took a dab of butter and put it in the frying pan. Then he went to the refrigerator to get some eggs. By the time he got back, the butter had turned brown. Paul didn't say anything, but Howie knew his brother would have had sense enough not to walk away and leave butter melting.

When he brought the eggs to the table, Paul poured a glass of milk for him.

"Was it nice?" Paul asked.

"Was what nice?"

"The sunrise."

"Oh, sure, swell." Howie was enjoying sitting with his big brother, even though this was his second batch of terrible-tasting eggs for the day. He wished he could tell Paul all about the strange men and the raft. If Paul helped them, they could make the best raft ever.

But he and the twins had agreed to keep it a secret. He changed the subject so he wouldn't say something by accident. "How did the baseball game go?" he asked.

Paul took a gulp of chocolate milk. "I struck out. We lost the game. Looks like the major league scouts won't be after me this year."

If there was one thing Howie envied about his brother, it was the way Paul didn't get excited when things went wrong. But then, if you were an honor student and high scorer on the basketball team, a little thing like striking out in a baseball game wouldn't bother you. Paul had a sort of margin for error—that was it. Howie had read that phrase someplace. As for himself, he sometimes thought, he had no margin. All he had were errors.

As if reading his mind, Paul said, "You're in trouble."

Howie felt his high spirits leaving him with wearying suddenness. This was the story of his life. "Why?" he asked.

"You left the kitchen in a mess," Paul began to recount.

"I was in a hurry," Howie explained. "I didn't want to be late for the sunrise."

"Logical," said Paul, "and forgivable. But why did you go away without saying where you were going? Didn't you know Mom and Dad would worry? Why didn't you leave a note?"

"I didn't think," Howie sighed.

"You never think," said Paul quietly.

"Well, maybe if I was a member of the National Honor Society and had a great big giant brain, I'd think," Howie flared up.

"Now, don't get sore," said Paul. "I understand how going to the river to watch the sun rise didn't seem to require a written explanation. But there's a rule around here—you and I both have to tell where we're going. You don't need to give complete details," Paul added hastily. "Just give a general idea of where you are going to be in case of an emergency."

Howie looked at him warily. "Suppose what you were doing was a secret. How can you tell about it without spoiling the secret?"

The toaster shot two pieces of toast up through its slots. Paul took one and handed one to Howie. "I told you," he said. "You don't have to explain every last little thing you are going to do. After all, you're twelve years old. Mom and Dad figure you have enough sense not to get into trouble. All they want from you is a general idea of where you are going to be."

Howie thoughtfully munched his toast. Sometimes it was handy to have a brother old enough to live half in the world of kids and half in the world of adults. Paul was sort of like an interpreter at the UN. And Howie certainly needed an interpreter sometimes to under-stand what adults wanted of him.

From what Paul was saying, the secret raft could be safe. It was all right to build one, provided that your folks knew you were at the river. But then, when it was time to take the raft to the swamp, would he have to ask permission for that?

Howie knew the answer and he didn't like it. No Thorneywoods parent in his right mind would give his child permission to go into the depths of the swamp-lands. Howie knew very clearly the correct thing to do. He should admit that Joel was right and call off the trip.

He dangled a piece of toast under the table as he thought of how he had bragged to the twins about being so brave. Pepper snapped the toast out of Howie's hands, almost taking along a finger. Joel and Diane looked up to him. They were about the only people who did. He wanted them to keep thinking he was brave. Then too, the more he thought about the swamp, the more he wanted to go there. It seemed like something he just had to do.

You might say that the swamp was really a part of the river. Therefore, if he had permission to go to the river, he had permission to go to the swamp. He wrinkled his brow. It sounded good, but there was something wrong with his reasoning.

"Something bothering you?" Paul asked curiously.

"No. Nothing at all," said Howie. He heard the sound of a car turning into the driveway. "There's Mom. Help me, will you, Paul, if she's still angry about this morning."

Mrs. Blake had the trunk of the car open, ready to take out the groceries, when the boys came out. Their sister Cindy had crawled into the trunk and was poking around in the bags.

"I want it," she pouted.

"Not now, Cindy," said Mrs. Blake. She turned to Howie. "Where were you?"

"He went to see the sun rise over the river," said Paul quickly. "He was in a hurry, or he would have left a note."

Suddenly Mrs. Blake smiled. "Did you see the sun rise?" she asked. "Wasn't it lovely? Daddy and I did that once when we were young. . . . Before you were born," she added.

Howie was a little surprised. He never thought people like mothers would be interested in sunrises.

As Mrs. Blake handed each boy a heavy package of groceries, she said severely, but not very angrily, "Howie, how many times do I have to tell you never to go anyplace without letting us know where you are?"

"I'm sorry," said Howie.

"Well," said his mother, "I can't let it go as easily as that. I think you'd better stay home tomorrow."

Howie almost sighed with relief. It could have been the whole holiday! Then, like the practiced punishment-bargainer he was, he said, "May the twins come over?"

"I guess so," his mother replied. "Cindy, I said no!"

But Cindy was already burrowing in a grocery bag still in the trunk. "I got it!" she yelled, fishing out a cereal box gleefully.

She climbed out of the trunk and opened the cereal box. Digging into the corn flakes, she drew out a little tin whistle shaped like an ear of corn. Then, with golden curls bobbing and fat little legs twinkling, she ran toward the house, blowing the whistle and spilling cereal flakes on the way.

"There goes the cereal," sighed Mrs. Blake as they walked toward the back door.

"The birds will like it," laughed Paul.

"Personally," said Mrs. Blake, "I think that brand of cereal *is* for the birds. It tastes like stale cardboard. I only bought it because Cindy saw it advertised on television and made such a fuss about the whistle in the package."

She opened the back door. "Good grief, look at the mess in this kitchen!"

"We'll clean it up," offered Howie.

As he and Paul washed their dishes and put away the groceries, Howie could hear yells coming from Cindy. She was having the whistle taken away until the next day as punishment for not listening to her mother.

Howie put a new package of frozen hamburgers into the freezer compartment of the refrigerator. That Cindy certainly was dumb. He could have told her from the very beginning that not listening to Mother would lead to having the whistle taken away.

Then he smiled to himself. Maybe that's what made Paul so smart about things. Maybe it was just being older.

3: The Raft

It rained the next day, so being confined to the house did not turn out to be such a bad punishment. Diane had gone to the movies with one of her friends, but Joel came anyway.

The boys settled themselves with a large bowl of fruit in the rainy-day corner of the basement, a cozy spot furnished with old tables and chairs, very good for planning a raft.

Howie took a pencil and a sheet of paper and started listing the things they would need: "Logs (cut from trees), saws, nails."

Then he put the pencil down. "Let's draw a picture first. My father never does anything down at the electronics plant without blueprints."

Joel wandered over to a bookcase holding an old set

of the encyclopedia. He flicked a finger over the backs of the volumes until he found "L." "Lumber would be in 'L,' " he said, leafing through the book. "Lumbermen always use rafts. Ah, here." He brought the book over to Howie and pointed to a picture.

Howie studied the illustration, showing lumbermen on a raft poling logs downriver. "The raft is bound together with twine or something," he pondered, as he started to draw.

"We need something very strong," Joel stated.

"I know!" Howie exclaimed. He ran over to his father's workshop and searched around in a dusty corner under the workbench. "Look!" he said triumphantly, drawing out a reel of copper wire.

"Hey, that's perfect," said Joel. "Are you sure your father won't mind our taking it?"

"He doesn't need it," said Howie. "It's left over from when he put the indirect lighting in the living room. That must have been three years ago."

Joel ran his fingers over the wire. "This stuff will cut our fingers when we wind it. We'll need gloves to work with it."

"Good idea," said Howie, and added "Copper wire" and "Gloves" to his list.

The boys each took a banana to help them think better and bent over the drawing again.

Howie wrinkled his brow. "Something bothers me."

"What?" asked Joel.

Frowning at the sketch he had drawn, Howie said, "No matter how tightly we wind the copper wire, there will be cracks between the logs for the water to come in."

Joel turned the sketch upside down, as if that would help him see the underside of the raft. "How about flat boards nailed to the bottom?"

"Hmm," said Howie, absent-mindedly putting his banana peels into a trash basket, "that should do the trick. But we'll need money to buy the boards."

"I have three dollars saved from my allowance," offered Joel. "And Diane has some baby-sitting money."

"Well," said Howie slowly, "I was saving up for some airplane models, but I guess this is more important."

He wrote down "Flat boards." Then he sat chewing on the pencil a moment. "We're going to need some calking compound to make sure she's watertight," he decided.

"We'd better measure," Joel reminded him. "We can't just walk into a lumber yard and ask for some boards. We have to know what length. Now let's see—there'll be three of us. We want to have plenty of room. . . ."

The boys spent the rest of the day figuring every detail, down to the last naïl. Early the next morning Howie packed his express wagon with copper wire, nails, saws, and hammers, closed the door firmly on Pepper, saying, "Sorry, boy, today you'd be in the way," and trundled the wagon down to the Matsons'. This time he remembered to leave a note telling his family he was going to the river.

Joel and Diane added more supplies, including lunch, to the load. With the express wagon bumping along behind, they made for their first stop, the supermarket. When they asked for some cartons, the manager simply waved a hand toward a bin of them. They selected three and took them out to the parking lot and cut them up into flat pieces. Then they stacked them in the express wagon and walked over to their next stop, Seaman's Lumber Yard.

At the clatter of the express wagon, Mr. Seaman, a tall, thin man with a drooping mustache, came ambling out of his office.

"Scrap pile's over in the shed," he said. "Take what you want, but don't bother the men working there." Mr. Seaman was used to having people come to him for odd pieces of lumber and dowels to use in school or Scout projects.

"We don't want scrap," said Howie importantly. "We want to buy some boards."

He handed Mr. Seaman the paper with the measurements written on it.

"Cash customers, eh?" said Mr. Seaman. He examined the paper with twinkling eyes. "Just hold on a few minutes. I'll have these cut up for you."

He disappeared into the shed and soon the three could hear the whine of the saw cutting up their boards. Then Mr. Seaman returned, carrying them.

"Here you are," he said, helping to stack the boards on the wagon. "Are you building a tree house?"

"No," said Joel, but Howie thought that sounded rather rude, so he offered, "More like a boat."

"Aha, a raft," Mr. Seaman grinned. "Built one myself when I was your age. Now, you be careful when you go out on that river. Stay close to shore."

"Why did you tell him our secret?" scolded Diane as they left the lumber yard.

"I didn't tell him. He guessed," said Howie defensively. "Anyhow, he doesn't know the secret part."

Joel looked at the boards approvingly. "Mr. Seaman's okay," he said. "He didn't cheat us on the wood. This is good stuff."

Howie reached over to restack a board that was falling off the wagon. "You know," he said dreamily, "we're really doing all this for people like Mr. Seaman. Can you imagine what would happen to his electric saw if we let those spies blow up the hydroelectric plant?"

As the words left Howie's mouth, they sounded silly to him. He realized he was just trying to talk himself into believing it was right to go to the swamp when he knew it was wrong.

The last stop was the nautical shop over near the docks. The dim, cool interior had an exciting feel to it. It was full of shiny outboard motors and deck paint and brightly colored kapok cushions and skin-diving equipment. There was an oily smell that made you think of summer days on the river.

"What'll it be, folks?" asked the proprietor, Mr. Gold.

"Can of calking compound," said Howie.

While Mr. Gold was getting the compound, Joel and Diane wandered off to look at all the interesting things in the store. Just as Howie was paying for the compound, he heard a cry from Joel.

"Look at that! Just what we need."

Howie hurried over to the corner where his friends were standing looking at a pile of junk. Joel was holding a pair of splintery canoe paddles, and Diane had found a broken-off oar.

"How much do you want for these?" they asked Mr. Gold.

"By gum, I didn't even know I had 'em," he said.

"Take the whole lot for a quarter and I'll thank you for it."

Howie found a quarter and they put their treasures in the express wagon, which was getting pretty tippy by now. Joel pulled it while Howie and Diane held on to the things to keep them from falling off. It was hard going when they reached the woods, but they finally had all their supplies in front of the hide-out.

"Now," said Howie, rubbing his hands with excitement, "all we have to do is to build the raft!"

First they lined the muddy ground of the hide-out with the dry cardboard and then they stowed away the supplies. Next came the search for logs.

It was amazing how many tree limbs were the wrong size for logs. In fact, it seemed that all the good limbs were way up high. But by climbing and hacking and sawing they managed to gather some logs and bring them back to the hide-out.

They laid the flat boards down side by side and set the logs on top of the boards. There weren't nearly enough to cover the boards, so out they went to the woods again for more sawing.

"This job is going to take longer than we thought," said Howie. "It'll take all day just to get enough logs."

The three settled down on the cardboard floor and opened the lunch bag.

"Have a ham sandwich," said Diane. "I wonder how the pioneers ever managed to make themselves log cabins."

Her brother and Howie took sandwiches and Joel said, "They had cabin-raising days when everyone chopped down trees. You know, I think we'd be better off working outside. I have a crick in my neck from stooping down in here, and it's dark."

They dragged the boards outside and, as Joel said, the work went faster. But it took all day to get the logs cut. At the end of it, they pushed everything back into the hide-out. Early the next day they came back to start nailing the boards together. They found they couldn't get them to stay smoothly, so they went back to Mr. Seaman with their problem. He suggested narrow wooden strips, called furring strips, that could be nailed under the boards. That worked fine, and by Thursday night they had made a sound, smooth platform on which to lay the logs.

On Friday they brought along some sandpaper and smoothed down the ragged ends of the logs. Then came the binding with copper wire. Tugging and hauling and grunting, the three of them finally managed to lash the logs together.

Carefully, they laid the planks on top of the logs, which were still pretty wiggly. Then they nailed and nailed and nailed.

"Remember that play we once did in second grade about the shoemaker and the elves?" giggled Diane.

The boys smiled. No matter what they did, Diane always remembered a story or a play that it recalled to her.

Joel stuck some nails in his mouth. "I'm the little shoemaker," he whistled through the nails.

Howie laughed, then growled, "Come off it, will you. We've got to get this thing finished. Tomorrow is the last day of vacation."

"Ugh," said Joel, taking the nails out of his mouth and starting to hammer again.

Finally they were satisfied that the planks were nailed down tightly. Then, with great heaving and tugging, they managed to turn the raft right side up. They all took a walk around it.

"That copper wire makes a pretty pattern, doesn't it," commented Diane.

But the boys were not interested in pretty designs. They wanted to make sure the raft wouldn't leak. They squeezed calking compound into every crack they could find. But still Howie had a worried look.

"I think we forgot something," he frowned.

The three scanned the raft carefully. It certainly looked sturdy, with the fat, round logs lined up so neatly and calking compound so lavishly applied to the cracks. But there was something. . . .

"I know," exclaimed Diane. "The bottom needs painting. You never have a raw wood bottom on a boat. It would get all water-soaked."

The boys had not lived next to the Deerlick River all their lives not to realize that Diane was right. They pooled the rest of their money and went to the hardware store, where they asked for deck paint.

"What color?" asked the proprietor.

Howie shrugged. "Doesn't matter. Gray, I guess."

"It does matter," said Diane indignantly. "We want something pretty. Now, what goes with brown logs . . . green, I guess. We want a nice shade of green, not too bright . . . something woodsy."

"Diane," sighed Joel, "we are painting a raft bottom, not decorating a living room."

The paint-store owner raised his hand. "The little lady is right. As long as you are going to paint, it might as well look nice. We have some green paint right here . . . goes beautifully with logs."

Diane's dark eyes glowed with pleasure in spite of the teasing. "You'll see. We'll paint the paddles to match."

After they had given the bottom of the raft two coats of green paint and painted the paddles, they had to admit Diane was right. The green paint gleamed in the sun and the paddles sparkled.

Diane clapped her hands. "It's the most beautiful raft I've ever seen."

Howie stood with his hands on his hips, just gazing at their creation. It was really here, whole and finished, the raft, their passport to adventure. Trying to keep his voice calm, he said, "All right, now, let's carefully put her into the hide-out to dry overnight. Then tomorrow we'll have the launching."

On Saturday morning they raced down to the hide-out and dragged out the raft. It was dry and ready to go.

"Come on, come on!" shouted Howie. "Let's get it in the water."

"Just a minute," said Joel. "She has to have a name."

They all sat down and thought.

"I know!" said Howie, getting to his feet. "A boat is a girl, so how about calling it the *Diane?*"

Diane's face turned a deep red. "Oh, no," she stammered.

"Don't be silly," said her brother briskly. "You helped make the raft. Why shouldn't it be named after you?" With a flourish, he picked up a paint brush, dipped it into the green paint, and wrote *Diane* on the end log.

He stepped back to admire his handiwork. "As soon as the name dries, we'll have a regular launching, like they have with a battleship. Diane, you'll do the launching."

"Oh," she said nervously, "I'll have to break a bottle of something over it. What if I miss?"

"You won't miss," said Howie confidently. "The only little thing we have to worry about is whether the

Diane floats once she's launched. Come on, let's go to the Coke machine on the dock and get a Coke bottle."

They trooped down to the dock, where Howie slipped a dime into the machine and drew out a bottle of Coke. With a flourish, he put it under the opener, nipped off the cap, and gave it to Diane.

"We'll all drink a toast to the *Diane,*" he said. "Ladies first."

Diane took a small swig. "To the *Diane,*" she giggled.

"Not like that," said Howie. "You have to give it 'oomph.'" He raised the Coke bottle and intoned, "To the good raft *Diane.* May she always sail in happy waters!" Then he took a deep drink. He was thirsty.

"Say, that was good," admired Joel. "Now it's my

turn." He reached for the bottle, raised it aloft, and shouted, " 'One for all, all for one,' like *The Three Musketeers!*" Then he drained the bottle down to the bottom.

"Now," said Howie, drawing a deep breath, "for the big test. Next stop the river."

Howie and Joel each took a corner of the raft and dragged it as Diane beat a pathway through the bushes.

"Boy, she sure is solid," puffed Howie.

"Maybe too solid," said Joel. "We might have made her too heavy to float."

As Joel planted that horrible thought in his mind, Howie became a little panicky. "Come on," he shouted. "Let's hurry." He wanted to get the suspense over with as soon as possible.

They kept on tugging and heaving until they got to the pebbly beach. Then the three of them dragged the raft the last few feet to the water's edge.

"Now!" said Howie nervously. "It's time for the launching. Okay, Diane."

His knees shook with nervousness as Diane filled the bottle with river water and raised it high above her head. "I christen thee *Diane*," she shouted in a quavering voice. Then she hurled the bottle of water onto the raft. The bottle splintered into a hundred pieces of glass and the water spilled over the end log.

"Wonderful," chattered Howie. "Now let's get her into the water. Brush off that glass there."

"Don't you think we ought to take off our shoes before we wade?" Joel suggested.

"Oh yes, of course," said Howie foolishly. He had

been ready to follow the raft into the water with his shoes and socks on.

"But watch out for the glass," said Joel.

Barefoot, they eased the raft into the water. The water was icy cold, but they hardly noticed. Finally the bottom of the raft cleared the sand. The three held it suspended in the shallow water.

"Let go," said Howie tensely.

Holding their breath, they let go. The *Diane* bobbed a little, then settled on top of the water.

"She's floating!" Howie cried joyfully.

He started to climb aboard. Joel followed. Diane ran back to the beach for the paddles and hoisted herself on too. The raft tipped on one side, but when they shifted around a bit, it righted itself.

The boys shoved off and the raft sailed out into the middle of the river. As Howie and Joel paddled in circles, Diane experimented with the broken oar, using it as a kind of rudder.

The captain of a tugboat pulling a barge blew his whistle at them and waved.

"Hi!" they shouted, and waved back.

Howie sat back in happy satisfaction and let his paddle trail in the water. He looked upriver toward Round Lake. There, beyond it, lay the swamp and adventure.

"Let's go to the swamp," he said eagerly.

Joel peered at the sun. It was already early afternoon. "Don't you think it's kind of late to be going to the swamp? We won't have time to really explore."

Howie looked at his friend keenly. He wondered

whether Joel was just making excuses. But he had to admit that Joel, as always, was being sensible. A trip to the swamp should really be made in the morning, with a full day ahead.

He glanced once again at the curving river, up toward the swamp. A beam of sunlight seemed to be pointing the way to the mystery.

"We have to go back to school Monday," he started to argue. "That means we have to wait until next Saturday. Maybe the spies will go away by then."

His words trailed away at the sight of Diane's face. She was with her brother. She just wasn't ready for the swamp right now. And even she didn't really believe the men were spies.

"All right," said Howie lamely. "We'll put it off until next Saturday. But," he continued defiantly, "if you don't want to go then, I'll go alone."

Joel smiled. "Don't be silly, Howie. Of course we want to go. Next Saturday morning, May 1, we'll go to the swamp. That's a date."

4: The Report

If Howie had ever felt that school was tiresome, it was nothing compared to how he felt that Monday. It was unbearable. The minutes moved on leaden feet as the class droned through the prepositions and reviewed the division of fractions.

He put his chin on his hand and stared out the window at the blue-and-green April day. There was just a sliver of river visible, but Howie could almost hear the splash of the water and feel the warm wooden paddle in his hand as the *Diane* set forth to adventure.

Vaguely he heard Mr. Frost announce that it was social studies time. He dug into his desk and pulled out his social studies book. A variety of rulers, pencils, and erasers clattered to the floor.

"Howard, if you kept your desk in reasonable order, you would not waste our time this way," said Mr. Frost.

Howie bent down and picked up the debris from the floor and stowed it back in the desk. He hadn't heard what page they were up to, so he peeked at the book of the girl sitting next to him. Page 235, the map of India. He opened the book and propped it in front of him with an angelic expression on his face.

"First we will have the Agriculture Report. Will the committee please come to the front of the room," said Mr. Frost.

The Agriculture Report! There was something familiar about that. Wildly, Howie's brain retraced history to pre-Easter vacation days. He was on the Indian Agriculture Committee!

Now he remembered dimly his mother telling him one day during vacation that George Nelson had called him to discuss a committee report. Howie had forgotten to call George back. Not only that, he had been so busy with the raft, it had never even occurred to him to go to the library to look up Indian agriculture in the encyclopedia.

He saw George get up, holding his neat report on "Rice." He saw Margaret O'Neil rise, carrying her neat report on "Cotton." Then, because Mr. Frost's eye was on him, he saw himself get up with no report, neat or otherwise, on "Implements of Agriculture."

As the committee members seated themselves on chairs in front of the class, Howie took the end seat. He figured if he came last he might learn something from the others—Howie had had previous experience with this kind of situation.

Mr. Frost had also had previous experiences with Howie.

"Howard, don't you have a written report?" he asked suspiciously.

"Oh, no," said Howie in what he imagined was his nonchalant voice. "I always like to do an oral report from memory. It's so much more . . . uh, more . . ."

"Spontaneous?" suggested Mr. Frost helpfully.

"Yes, that's it," Howie agreed. "Spontaneous." He filed the word away in his mind under "useful information." "Spontaneous." A very good word when you were not prepared. It might come in handy again some time. Then he looked at Mr. Frost's face. Spontaneous wouldn't come in handy in Mr. Frost's classroom again, that was sure.

The committee settled down and George started giving the first report. Howie listened frantically for stray bits of information as George droned away about rice paddies. Then Margaret, with dramatic expression, read her report about India's cotton fields. Again Howie listened intently, grasping ideas for his spontaneous unprepared talk about Indian agricultural implements.

Then Mr. Frost said pleasantly, "Howard, we're ready for you."

Howie almost said, "So soon?" but restrained himself. He got to his feet nervously and gulped like a newly caught fish. A giggle was heard from the back of the room. Joel abruptly propped a social studies book in front of his face. Howie was thankful that Diane was in another sixth-grade class.

"Well," he began, "the Indian people do a lot of farming. They like to farm. That is how they get their food.

But they don't kill the cows, so they don't eat steaks like
we do." He remembered this from a film strip.

"Howie," said Mr. Frost patiently, "please stick to
your subject, 'Agricultural Implements.'"

"Uh, yes," Howie continued. "Well, as you know, the
Indians plant cotton in some parts of their country. For
this they need cotton gins and cotton pickers." This bit
of information came from a fifth-grade unit on "The
Southern States." Howie was glad he hadn't forgotten
about that.

But Mr. Frost said, "Excuse me for interrupting, Howard. I thought we had made it clear that Indian farming is very primitive. That's their big problem."

"Oh," said Howie. "They don't have cotton gins. They don't have cotton pickers. They just plant the cotton and pick it and take the seeds out all by themselves, by hand."

Anxiously, he glanced at Mr. Frost. Mr. Frost was twiddling his red pencil. He seemed to be counting to himself very softly, "One, two, three, four."

Howie drew a deep breath. Well, he had taken care of the cotton fields. Now for the rice.

"They grow rice," he said confidently, remembering George's report. "They grow it in the hot, wet areas. To grow rice they, uh, use rice paddies. As the rice grows, the Indians go around patting it with the paddies."

"Eight, nine, ten!" said Mr. Frost loudly. The class was in an uproar of laughter. "Haw, haw, haw," shouted Ralph Murphy, slapping his knee.

"Sit down, Howard," Mr. Frost ordered.

As Howie returned to his seat, the knowledge hit him like a bomb that rice paddies are the wet bogs where rice is grown. He slumped down in his seat and grinned at his giggling classmates, trying to make them think he was just trying to be funny.

Mr. Frost jumped up and energetically started handing out paper. Then he rapidly wrote some addition examples on the board.

"You've all been getting very careless with simple arithmetic lately," he said with sudden heartiness. "This is a good time for a drill. Now, I want you to check each example carefully. Go over it twice, three times if necessary," he added enthusiastically.

The room subsided as if by magic. After all, it is almost impossible to laugh while you are checking an addition example three times.

Howie stole a look at Joel's face. He looked worried. As if by mental telepathy, Howie followed what his friend was thinking. Joel was foreseeing the normal turn of events resulting from Howie's performance.

First there would be, inevitably, a scene with Mr.

Frost. Then Mr. Frost would do something. Howie tried to put himself in Mr. Frost's place. What would he do if he were the teacher? He would inform the boy's parents. Howie started to shiver at the next question. What would the parents do? They would punish, and it wouldn't be any one-day restriction, either.

As Howie turned the prospects over in his mind, they all came to one nightmarish conclusion—the punishment was going to prevent him from going to the river. The *Diane* would never take her adventure trip into the swamp!

His heart sank. He spent the rest of the afternoon in silent misery.

When the dismissal bell rang, Mr. Frost motioned for him to stay. Joel tactfully left with the rest of the class, making hand signals to let Howie know he'd meet him outside.

Mr. Frost came back from the hall after seeing that the class didn't run down the stairs like a herd of elephants. He strode over to his desk and sat down. Howie stood before him, feeling like a murderer awaiting the judge's sentence.

Mr. Frost leaned back and clasped his stomach, like a kindly old professor on television. Only Mr. Frost wasn't old. In fact, he was very young. He had hardly any stomach to clasp. But he tried to look wise and kindly anyhow.

He gazed at Howie with distressed brown eyes. Howie shifted uneasily.

"I don't know what to do with you," said the teacher in a rather phony-sad voice. "It isn't as if you don't have the ability. . . ."

Howie waited. He had been through all this before, with other teachers. Only the other teachers usually tried to stay wise and kindly. Mr. Frost now straightened up, dropped the act, and shot at Howie with a hard, tough voice, "Why didn't you do the report?"

"I just didn't have the time," Howie muttered.

"Everyone else had the time," Mr. Frost rasped.

This was a fact. Howie said nothing.

Mr. Frost drew a clean piece of paper toward him and rapped on it with his pen. "Shall I drop a note to your parents about this?"

"Oh, please, don't do that," Howie begged. "My mother has been so tired and overworked lately. I wouldn't want to bother her."

Mr. Frost's eyes were still hard, but he didn't uncap the pen. "What makes you think you can get away with not doing the work everyone else does?" he demanded.

Howie squirmed a little. Then he blurted out, "Please, Mr. Frost, give me another chance. I'll write a report. I'll do a big report, ten pages."

"Fifteen," said Mr. Frost severely. He tapped the piece of note paper again with his pen.

"Fifteen," echoed Howie dismally.

"On my desk Friday morning," Mr. Frost ordered.

Howie thought of something. "If the Indians don't have many agricultural implements, how can I write fifteen pages about it?"

Mr. Frost smiled. "You have a point, Howard. How about changing your topic to something that has a lot to it . . . say, "The Religions of India and Pakistan"? That would be Hinduism and Mohammedanism."

Howie sighed. He had the feeling that Mr. Frost had

tricked him into something. "Okay," he said. " 'Religions of India and Pakistan,' fifteen pages, on your desk Friday morning. You can depend on me, Mr. Frost."

"I hope so, Howard," said Mr. Frost. "I sincerely hope so."

Howie darted out of the school building and met Joel, waiting anxiously at the entrance. "You've got to help me," he said. "We have to go to the Thorneywoods Public Library and find everything they have on Hinduism and Mohammedanism. I've got to get fifteen pages on the subject to Mr. Frost by Friday morning or we can kiss our trip to the swamplands good-by."

Howie and Joel rushed over to the library. They looked the two religions up in the card catalog. Then they started grabbing the books they needed off the shelves. The librarian gave Howie a funny look and told him he could only take six books home. The boys leafed through the books and picked the six they thought were best.

Joel helped Howie carry the books home, then left him alone with a stack of empty note cards, some clean sheets of paper, and four days in which to write fifteen pages.

Howie stared at the tower of books. The job looked impossible to him. He shrugged, sharpened a pencil, and began.

He remembered that Mr. Frost had told the class always to break up a topic into parts. Howie thought about his topic a while. Then he started labeling his note cards: "Beliefs," "History," "Training of Children."

After that, the project became a kind of game. He tried to see how many facts he could find for each subject. As the note cards started to fill up, Howie became more and more interested. He was working so hard, he was amazed when he was called for dinner.

As soon as dinner was over he raced upstairs to do some more detective work on his subject and kept at it until his father had to remind him to go to bed.

On Tuesday night Howie finished taking notes. On Wednesday he started writing. He wrote and he wrote and he wrote. Everything seemed too important to leave out. His family tiptoed around him in astonished silence. They had no idea what was making him work so hard, but they certainly didn't want to spoil it.

Finally Paul was appointed by the family to find out, tactfully, what it was all about.

"What's with this writing bit?" he asked. "Are you going to stay up all night? It's after ten."

"Um," said Howie absently. He was in the middle of writing about the religious war between the Hindus and the Mohammedans that had caused India to split into two countries, India for the Hindus and Pakistan for the Mohammedans. It was very exciting and he didn't like being interrupted.

Paul picked up a few sheets and started reading. "Hey, this is good stuff," he said. "This is good enough for a high school report. Do you have a bibliography?"

"What's that?" Howie asked, his face burning with pleasant embarrassment at his brother's praise.

"It's a list of your references; name of book, author, and publisher, and the year the book was published."

"Oh, that," said Howie. "I haven't gotten around to that yet."

He looked at the sheet on which he was working and

noted to his amazement that he was already up to Page 16. The report was already longer than it had to be and it wasn't nearly done. Suddenly he felt very tired and he yawned.

"Why don't you knock off for tonight?" Paul advised. "You'll see, the work will go better tomorrow."

The next day Howie stopped at a stationery store and bought a blue report folder. His report was going to be a giant one, longer than any that had ever been handed in in his class, and he wanted it to look right.

He sat down at his desk Thursday evening, knowing that he had to finish even if it took all night. But when he started working, the words seemed to fly under his pen. He knew exactly what he was going to say. It seemed no time at all until he was finished.

He remembered what Paul had told him about listing his references. On the top of a clean page he wrote "Bibliography." Then he listed the six books, their authors, publishers, and years. It looked very official.

He inserted the pages into the report folder, neatly lettered the title on the cover, and stepped back to admire it. It was beautiful. Twenty pages bulged fatly inside the folder. Howie couldn't wait to see how astounded Mr. Frost would be and how foolish the rest of the class would feel for having laughed at him.

He came to school early the next day. Approaching the teacher on hall duty, he announced that he had an important errand to do for Mr. Frost. She looked at him skeptically, but finally let him into the building.

Walking quietly along the dim corridors, he stayed close to the wall so he wouldn't be noticed. As he passed the cafeteria he saw Mr. Frost having his morning coffee with the other teachers. Just then Mr. Frost got up as if he were about to leave.

Howie hurried down the hall to his classroom as fast as he could without running. It was silly, he knew, but he just didn't want to meet Mr. Frost. He wanted to put the report on the teacher's desk and run away.

The knob on the door did not turn. Howie's heart sank. The door was locked. Then he heard footsteps behind him and turned.

Mr. Frost was standing there. He looked very angry. "What are you doing here, Howard?" he asked coldly. "Don't you know you are not supposed to be in the building before 8:45?"

The tall young teacher towered over Howie as few people did. As Howie looked up at him, his face went pale, even under the freckles around his nose.

"Er," he said, "I . . . er . . . just wanted to give you this."

He thrust the report at Mr. Frost. The teacher automatically reached out for it. Then he looked around. But Howie was gone, running down the hall toward the outside door as fast as he could go.

When the class came in, Mr. Frost barely said "Good morning." He was sitting at his desk bent over Howie's report. John Moore, the attendance monitor, took the attendance. The pledge leader led the Pledge of Allegiance. Mr. Frost just got up briefly to salute the flag; then he sat right down and kept on reading.

"Turn to page 154 in your spelling books," he said absently, "and write a good sentence for each word."

Several students began to protest that they had already done that on Tuesday, that Friday was test day, not sentence-writing day.

"Write new sentences," growled Mr. Frost. "You need the practice."

The students shrugged and started writing spelling sentences. Mr. Frost hunched over Howie's report again. Howie obediently opened his spelling workbook like the rest of the class and started writing sentences. But he kept one eye on Mr. Frost, almost wild with curiosity at what the teacher thought of the report. But Mr. Frost said nothing.

At recess, Mr. Frost said very quietly, "Howard."

This was the usual summons when Mr. Frost wanted to talk to a student privately about his work. Howie walked to the teacher's desk.

Mr. Frost pushed the closed report aside, leaned back in his chair, and asked Howie some questions. They were about the religions of India and Pakistan. It seemed like an oral test. Howie answered the questions quickly. He knew the answers very well. After all, he had just written a report on the subject.

Then Mr. Frost drew the report forward and opened it to the first page. He took his red pencil and wrote "A-plus Outstanding."

Howie gulped. He had never received a mark like that in his life.

Mr. Frost spoke. His voice sounded strangely husky. "I want to apologize to you, Howie," he said.

Howie said nothing. He was just as surprised at Mr. Frost's calling him "Howie" as at what he said.

"I asked you these questions," continued Mr. Frost,

"because I doubted that you could have written this report yourself. You showed me you knew the material and I am ashamed of having doubted you."

"That's all right," said Howie. "I would have felt the same way, considering the work I've been doing."

"No, it's not all right," insisted Mr. Frost. "You have been in my class for eight months. I should have known what you are capable of doing."

He tapped the report with his finger. "This means a lot more than an A-plus in social studies for you, Howie. It proves something I've been trying to convince the Thorneywoods school people of, that some sixth-graders must be given harder work in order to keep them interested."

Looking at Howie very intently, he said, "I'm going out on a limb about something. I'm going to send this report down to the principal with the recommendation that you be placed in the accelerated seventh grade in junior high school. When Mr. Dunham looks at your grades, he'll probably tell me I'm not very well." His voice became slow and very serious. "Howie, at that point I want to be able to tell Mr. Dunham that I personally guarantee you will do nothing but A work in every subject for the rest of the year. Do I dare make that statement?"

Howie drew a deep breath. Promising perfect work was a tall order. He could not make a fool of Mr. Frost. Yet he knew schoolwork was easy for him when he paid attention. The trouble was that he never paid attention. "I'll try," he promised. "I won't let you down, Mr. Frost."

Mr. Frost smiled. "Don't get your hopes up too high.

I doubt whether I can convince Mr. Dunham. Above all, don't repeat this to anyone, not even your parents."

Howie went out to the playground feeling as if his shoes had rubber balloons in them. All day he walked around feeling dizzy with shock. Mr. Frost thought he was bright enough to go into the advanced class in junior high school, just as Paul had done!

Nothing more was said about the report. But Howie didn't care that the rest of the class didn't share his triumph. To Joel's eager questions after school, he merely replied that Mr. Frost had liked the report. He wanted to keep the secret to himself, inside, like a bright Christmas tree ornament he could take out and examine from time to time.

Meanwhile, he had something else to think about. Tomorrow was Saturday, the day he was going to the swamp. His stomach contracted a little with fear now that the time was so close, and he half hoped it would rain.

But he knew going to the swamp was something he had to do, just as when he wrote the report, it was a test of himself, something he had to do even though he was just a little afraid of doing it.

5: The Swamp

Very early Saturday morning Howie slipped out the back door and closed it firmly in Pepper's face. He could hear the dog whining in outraged disappointment at being left behind again, but this was one day Howie could do without his company. Whatever Pepper's fine qualities, Howie didn't know whether he'd be much of a sea dog.

He picked up Joel and Diane at their house and the three raced down to the river bank. It was real New England first-of-May weather. The air had a transparent light coolness and smelled of growing things. Fat little green balls of leaves had opened up during the week. Running under the trees was like going under a shimmering green ceiling.

They slid down the bank and made their way to the hide-out. There was the *Diane,* lying in the shadows, ready for her first real voyage.

Eagerly, they pulled the raft out and dragged it down to the water. Then they all gave it a good push and scrambled aboard.

"This is great," babbled Howie as they headed up the river. "I feel like Columbus."

"Look out!" shouted Joel. "Ship ahoy!"

A motorboat was bearing down on them. Hastily the boys paddled out of the way. The motorboat came tearing past and splashed them.

"Some people just don't show any consideration," muttered Howie, brushing the water off his shirt. "Gosh, don't you wish we had a motorboat?"

"No," said Joel. "A motorboat wouldn't be good for our purpose."

"What purpose?" asked Howie.

"Sneaking up on the spies," said Joel seriously. "If we had a motorboat, they would hear us."

Howie dipped his paddle into the water thoughtfully. "Joel," he said, "do you really believe those men were spies?"

"No," Joel admitted. "I think they were fishermen. They probably didn't even go to the swamp."

"Then why are we going there?" Diane demanded, her hand shaking as she guided her broken oar. "The swamps are spooky. Anyhow, I don't think our parents would like it."

"That's true," admitted Howie. "I don't think our parents would like it. The only reason I'm going to the swamps is because they are there and I've never seen the inside of them. But we can just take a little ride to Round Lake and go back home if you'd rather."

Diane examined her old oar carefully. Then she jutted out her small, pointed chin. "No," she said. "We started out for the swamp. I think we should finish what we started."

"What do you think, Joel?" Howie asked.

"I don't think there's any harm if we just go in a little way and come right out again," Joel decided, somewhat unwillingly.

"Okay," said Howie. "It's agreed. Swamp, here we come."

They paddled a while in silence. Then Diane shouted, "Hey, what's that thing bobbing about in the water?" She pointed to what looked like a small black rock coming toward them from the shore.

Howie followed Diane's pointing finger. Strange, the rock seemed to have ears. Then it developed a shiny nose. It couldn't be . . . but it was . . . Pepper!

"Stop paddling," he directed Joel. "Someone must have let that hound out and he's following me."

"Look at that pooch swim," said Joel admiringly. "It must be a half mile from shore."

Howie's annoyance turned to affection as he watched the little dog painfully and steadily paddling through the water, his paws churning up and down like pistons. That dog would keep on coming if he drowned trying!

They turned the raft around and paddled toward the dog. When they reached him, Howie pulled him, dripping wet, onto the raft. Pepper shook himself, spraying everyone, and staggered over to Howie with that "Aren't you glad to see me?" look in his eyes. He wagged his tail with a couple of polite thumps. Then he lay down, his fat stomach heaving up and down with exhaustion. Howie took out his handkerchief and rubbed the dog's soaking hide.

"Good boy," he said. "Good Pepper."

The tail thumped again wearily. Pepper closed his eyes and promptly started snoring.

They turned the raft back in the direction of the swamp; somehow, Howie felt less nervous with Pepper aboard. First they passed under the steel network of the bridge, with the roar of traffic overhead. Then they glided past the commercial docks of Sumner, swarming with barges and busy little tugs. The excursion steamer, newly painted red and white for the spring season, puffed along gaily with music playing. The passengers waved at them from the decks and they waved back.

Howie and Joel had to work hard with their paddles to keep the raft from bobbing around too much in the wake of all the traffic. Diane bent over the "rudder," twisting it back and forth. Only Pepper rested, sleeping peacefully.

After they passed Sumner, they came to quieter waters as the river widened out to placid Round Lake. The beach was deserted so early in the season. The only other people on the lake were teen-agers in two canoes, who seemed to be racing.

Looming above Round Lake was the wall of the dam, a rock and earth structure about twenty feet high. On top of the dam, although hidden, was the reservoir where the tumbling waters of the Deerlick coming down from the mountain were caught. A series of pipes let the water out on either side of the dam, falling in gentle streams into Round Lake. At the side of the reservoir, perched like a huge white bubble on the mountain, was the hydroelectric plant where the force of the river was turned into electricity.

Passing the dam, they looked up, as they always did, in silent awe. The people of Thorneywoods never forgot that it was the dam that kept the rushing waters from their town.

After paddling around the rim of Round Lake they came to a small stream leading to the swamp.

"Here goes," said Howie, swallowing hard.

Diane expertly maneuvered the oar while the two boys headed the raft into the stream. They paddled along in silence in the midst of an overgrown wilderness of trees and cattails. The stream was choked with growing things; they had to thrash away at weeds and duck under overhanging branches.

At first the water was clear. Then it grew muddier, and scummy. Pepper woke up and prowled around the raft, sniffing suspiciously.

The big trees seemed to get smaller and sickly-looking. It was very quiet. Even the bird songs had disappeared.

Then the stream ended abruptly in a lake.

"Wow!" cried Howie.

"It gives me the creeps," shuddered Diane.

Pepper growled.

The scene before them looked like a setting for a movie about the end of the world. It was a lake of drowned trees, gaunt dead trunks, and lifeless branches standing in motionless green slime. Above all was the silence, the complete and timeless silence.

"Let's get out of here," whispered Diane.

Howie dipped his paddle timidly into the green muck. His curiosity about the dead forest overcame his fear. "We'll go in just a little way," he said. "Then we'll turn around and go home."

As the raft glided through the eerie forest, the boys gripped the paddles hard. Suddenly they heard a sharp grating sound.

"Look out!" shouted Howie.

"It's a tree under the water," said Joel.

Rapidly, they paddled away from the submerged tree trunk. Then Pepper barked sharply at something beneath the surface. Howie dipped in his paddle. A cloud of mud rose from the bottom of the lake. Through the muck he could see a school of little silver fish.

"Quiet!" he ordered the dog. "Do you want to upset the raft?"

At his own words, the idea of being dumped into the green water entered Howie's mind. It certainly looked unpleasant. There was no telling how deep it was. Maybe the bottom was quicksand.

"Had enough?" he asked his companions with forced cheerfulness.

The twins nodded vigorously.

"There's the creek we came from," Joel pointed.

Hastily they headed the raft toward the creek and paddled down the stream to Round Lake. They wanted to get out of this place as soon as possible.

Then the creek came to a dead end.

"It was the wrong creek," said Howie.

The twins stared at him. They could see that.

They paddled back to the lake and looked around. It

seemed to stretch for miles, an endless procession of broken trees and slimy green water. A sour smell came from the scummy depths.

"Oh, we made a mistake. It was that creek over there," said Howie, pointing to the left.

They paddled into the other creek. After a few yards, that, too, came to an abrupt end.

Back at the lake again, they scanned the shore. It seemed as if there were outlets every few yards just like the one from which they had come. It would take hours to try each of them.

There was no sound except for the splash of the paddles and the slight tinkle of Pepper's dog license.

Then Howie had a thought. "I remember," he said. "The sun was behind us. All we have to do is to paddle toward the sun."

A cool wind crackled through the dead trees, but the three were hot with perspiration as they pointed their raft toward the sun.

But Howie's plan only led them to more dead-end creeks.

Joel was chewing his lip as if it were a piece of taffy. Diane's face was chalk white and her hand holding the oar was trembling. In another moment she was going to burst into tears.

Howie began to feel sick at his stomach. He knew the fault was his for this situation. He had insisted the others come to the swamp.

Overcome with his own stupidity, he hated himself for not having thought out this project sensibly before they started. All the good feeling he had had after his talk with Mr. Frost disappeared. He was just an idiot who kept doing things without thinking.

"Let's try the other side," said Diane in a voice she was trying to keep from sounding squeaky. "Maybe the sun moved."

Howie laughed with sudden relief. "Of course," he said. "Why didn't we think of that? The sun is in a different part of the sky than it was when we came in here. Let's look on the other side of the lake."

Cautiously they skirted around the shore, pushing away a netting of old plants and sticky mud. Again and again they paddled into new outlets. But they all led to dead ends.

Hopelessly, they drifted out to the center of the lake. By this time the raft was damp and muddy from the splashing paddles. Their legs were cramped from crouching on the small space. At this point they would have settled gladly for a dry place to land. But the shore all around was just an oozy mire. They were afraid if they beached the raft, they would not be able to get it loose.

Diane started to cry silently, the tears just rolling down her cheeks. The boys just stared at each other. No one spoke.

Suddenly Pepper growled, low in his throat. Howie felt a chill go up and down inside him. Pepper didn't growl very often. It was ridiculous, but maybe some prehistoric monster could be lurking in the swamp's slimy depths.

Then the object of Pepper's attention flew by. It was an enormous gray bird. It swished over to a tree branch and started to caw in a grating voice. Pepper looked up at it and yelped.

The children stared at the bird.

"Wow!" said Joel. "He's a big one."

Howie was too downcast to point out to Joel that the bird, at second glance, was not really unusually large. It was only that it was the only bird within miles.

A thought struck him. "From what direction did that bird come?" he suddenly demanded.

Joel hesitated, thinking. Then he pointed. "From over there," he said. "I remember seeing him come."

"Let's head for there," said Howie urgently.

"Why?" asked Diane.

"Birds don't nest in dead trees," Howie reasoned. "There must be dry land in that direction, with growing trees. At least we'd be able to beach the raft and get our bearings."

So they paddled as hard as they could in the direction from which the bird had come.

"Look!" shouted Howie, pointing his paddle toward land.

The lake had narrowed down into a creek. It wasn't the one through which they had come, but it wasn't a dead end, either. In the distance they could see the green of growing things.

They speeded up their paddling. First they steered through a pool of cattails. Then the stream narrowed down again and became deeper. The water started to get clearer. Sand, instead of mud, appeared on the banks. Tall maples and oaks, blessedly alive with green leaves, lined them. Andromeda, their white flowers cool and waxy, dipped over the water. The chirp of nesting birds was everywhere.

All three breathed a sigh of relief. They were still lost, but it was hard to stay worried in this lovely place.

6: The Island

"Let's go ashore," said Joel.

They steered over to the shore, jumped off the raft, and pulled it up onto the little sandy beach. Then they hopped up and down trying to get the kinks out of their legs. Pepper dashed into the bushes and ran around madly. After a few moments he came back and looked at Howie as if to say, "What's next?"

Howie scanned the forest. "There must be a way out of these woods leading to civilization."

"We could even camp out here," said Diane cheerfully. "Sooner or later people would come looking for us."

"We'd better blaze a trail," said Howie as they started into the woods. "We wouldn't want to lose the raft."

Joel took out his small pocket knife and made nicks in

the tree trunks as they walked past. It was soon clear, however, they couldn't get very lost here. They were on an island, and not a very large one. From every side they could see the glint of water through the trees.

With Howie in the lead, they made their way through the brambly underbrush. Howie pushed away an overhanging vine, then stopped so short the others collided with him.

"What's the matter?" they asked.

Without a word Howie pointed his finger, his hand shaking, toward a beach on the other side of the island.

There, tied to a tree, was a boat rocking gently in the water. It was a motorboat, once painted gray, but now rather grimy and peeling.

"It's . . . it's the spies' boat," stuttered Diane.

The children crept forward. Pepper tried to surge ahead, but Howie grabbed his collar. As they came to the edge of the woods, Howie motioned to the others to stoop down out of sight behind a bush. They crouched down and peeked through the bush. Up ahead rose the white peak of a tent.

"Shhh," said Howie. "I hear something."

They lay down, trying to keep their hearts from thumping so loudly. Pepper squirmed and whimpered in Howie's grasp until Howie clamped his hand over the dog's mouth.

Quite clearly, the sound of a radio came to them. They heard a queer jumble of words: "Abob-bob-bob a-foo-foo-foo."

"It's a code," whispered Joel. "They're receiving a message."

"To music?" wondered Howie.

"Sure, to music," said Diane. "That just makes it harder to intercept. I wish I understood their language."

Howie listened intently. Somehow, the code sounded familiar to him. Then he started to giggle softly. "I understand it," he said.

The others looked at him in astonishment. "You do?"

"Sure," he said. "You're so excited you don't even know what you're listening to."

The twins listened again. Then Joel laughed too. "That's the 'Larry Kay and his Hey Hey Hey' program."

"It's *Bob bob, bob, foo, foo, I love you!*" exclaimed Diane. "Number one on this week's Teen Parade of Hits."

Suddenly Howie fell over backward as the buckle of Pepper's collar gave way and the dog leaped forward. Pepper scampered through the woods toward the tent.

"Oh, brother," grumbled Joel. "That's all we need."

Loud exclamations were heard from the direction of the tent.

"Look Bud, a lost dog."

"Poor little fellow. He looks starved. Here boy, want a piece of steak?"

"They speak very good English," Howie commented.

"Of course," said Joel. "These spies train for years."

The smell of steak that had attracted Pepper began to drift back to the children. Howie felt an angry rumble from his empty stomach.

They could hear Pepper yipping pitifully. Then there was another, "Here, boy," and silence as Pepper devoured the meat.

"Those men will be lucky to have any steak left after Pepper gets through with them," said Howie.

Diane put a finger to her lips. "Listen!"

"Say, Bud," one of the men was saying, "this is a queer place to find a lost dog. There isn't a house on this island."

"That's right, Tom," said another voice. "Someone must have brought him here."

Then a new voice entered the conversation. "What's this, boys? Where did this dog come from? Here, fella. The poor thing looks starved."

Another pitiful wail from Pepper. Then the new voice said, "All right, boy. Here's a piece of steak for you."

"Lucky Pepper," murmured Howie. All this steak talk was getting to be too much for him.

"Dr. Stevens," said the voice that the children recognized as Bud's, "we think his owner must be on the island. See, he's lost his collar. The owner must be looking for him."

"Come on, boy," came the urging voice of Tom. "Let's find your master. Bud, give me a piece of steak so he'll follow me."

There were sounds of crackling through bushes, then a lighter crackle that could only come from the dog's paws. Joel started to hide behind a tree, but Howie stopped him.

"They'll find us anyway. We don't want them to know we were watching them. Let's just stay in the path as if we were looking for the dog."

They didn't have long to wait until Pepper came bounding through the bushes and rushed over to Howie. He was followed by the sharp-faced young man with glasses they had seen loading the boat the first day.

"Hello," said the young man with a friendly smile. He didn't look guilty or angry, the way you'd expect a spy to look. In fact, with his crew-cut blond hair and long skinny legs, he might have been one of Paul's teen-age friends, only a bit older.

The young man glanced at the empty collar in Howie's hand. "Dog broke loose, eh?"

"Yes," Howie replied. "He must have smelled your steak."

Immediately he felt like clamping his hand over his mouth. If he knew about the steak, the young man would realize they had been eavesdropping.

But he didn't seem to notice. He just continued in his friendly way, "My name is Tom Reynolds. Come and meet my friends."

There was nothing the children could do but follow him toward the tents. When they came to the cleared space in the woods occupied by the two white tents, they noticed a radio antenna projecting from one of them. Joel nudged Howie and nodded toward it.

In front of one of the tents, the short gray-haired man and the other young man they remembered were broiling steak over an open fire. A transistor radio was blasting away another hit tune of the week.

"Here's the dog's master," announced Tom, ushering Howie and the twins forward.

"His name is Pepper," offered Howie. He didn't know what else to say, but it seemed to him that if the men were going to give the dog half their meal, they should at least know his name.

The gray-haired man tickled Pepper behind the ears. "Hello, kids," he said. "I'm Dr. Stevens and this is Bud Calhoun."

Bud, a round-faced young man with black hair that had a way of falling down over his forehead, raised the frying pan in greeting, as the children told their names.

"Hi," he said. "Have a seat."

The three perched shyly on a large rock near the fire.

"How about some steak?" asked Bud.

The three tried not to reply too eagerly, although they felt as if they were perishing with hunger.

"Are you sure you have enough?" Diane asked politely.

"Certainly," smiled Tom. "We have a freezer full of steaks. I'll go get another one."

He went into one of the tents and brought out some tin plates, silverware, and another steak, which was soon sizzling over the fire. When it was done, he sliced off pieces onto everyone's plate. Dr. Stevens took a long-handled fork and fished baked potatoes out of the ashes.

"Mickeys," he explained. "That's what you call potatoes baked in the ashes. Like them?"

"Terrific!" the three agreed. This was beyond a doubt the most delicious meal they had ever eaten.

Suddenly Joel asked, "How can you run a freezer way out in the woods?"

Howie looked up sharply from his plate. Joel had been eying the antenna and now he was fishing for information. Howie was worried—Joel could make the men angry with questions like this.

But Bud just answered blandly, "We have a small generator that gives us electricity for refrigeration, electric lights, and whatever else we need. All the comforts of home."

But Bud's apparent friendliness did not quite still Howie's uneasiness. Ever since his remark about the potatoes, Dr. Stevens had lapsed into a deep silence, peering at the children from under his bushy gray eyebrows.

Howie tried not to stare at the older man, but Dr. Stevens seemed more and more mysterious every minute. There was something funny about his hands. He had long, rather knobby fingers. When he ate, they moved a knife and fork as if a precision machine were regulating them. Each piece of meat was cut swiftly, with a light delicacy, into perfect little cubes. And all this was done without Dr. Stevens looking at what he was doing; his blue eyes remained fixed on the children.

Bud offered Howie a piece of bread, but he declined with a shake of his head—he had lost his appetite.

He glanced at Joel and Diane. They were eating away as if food were going out of style. They hadn't even noticed the sinister expression on the doctor's face.

Alone in his panic, Howie reasoned that Dr. Stevens was probably wondering what to do with them. Maybe they'd be held for ransom. Or more likely, he was figuring out a way to get rid of them that would look like an accident. It would be easy in this swamp. If these men were spies, it wasn't reasonable to expect them to let three children go back to town with their story.

Just as Howie was getting so clammy with fear he didn't think he could stand it, Dr. Stevens finally spoke. He did not sound friendly.

"How did you get here?" He shot the question at the children accusingly.

Howie looked at the twins. He saw that his fear had spread itself to them as if borne on a radio wave.

"Er . . ." quavered Joel, "we came on a raft."

"Yes," said Howie, trying to sound agreeable, although he was terrified too. "It's beached on the other side of the island."

Dr. Stevens put his knife down. "Do you mean to tell me you ventured into this swamp alone?"

"Yes sir," said Howie faintly.

"If you had not found us, do you think you would have known how to get back?"

"We were lost," Diane admitted.

"Did your parents give you permission to go to the swamp alone?" Dr. Stevens demanded in a slightly louder voice.

"Our parents knew we went to the river," said Howie uncomfortably.

Suddenly he began to be conscious of a new feeling. He tried to put his finger on it. Then it came to him. It was like the sensation you have when you come in from outdoors on a nasty day and the warmth of the house finally gets to you and you begin to lose your chill.

What was it about Dr. Stevens' manner that had made the strangeness slip away? All at once Howie realized he was in the midst of a discussion with the gray-haired stranger that was exactly like the discussions he always had with his father or Mr. Frost when he had been caught doing something wrong.

"But did you tell them you were going to the swamp?" Dr. Stevens persisted.

Howie almost laughed. The very tone of Dr. Stevens'

voice sounded like his father's. Dr. Stevens couldn't possibly be a spy. If he were, he'd be more interested in his secret plans than in scolding children for foolish behavior.

"No, sir," Howie mumbled. He knew he was backed into a corner, just as he generally was with his father. But he didn't mind.

He didn't even mind when Dr. Stevens thundered, "Do you realize how dangerous and thoughtless your adventure was? Suppose you had not found us? It might have been days before anyone located you. Think of the fright you would have given your parents!"

"I'm sorry, sir. We just didn't think," Howie said solemnly.

Although this was the sort of thing he always said when a scolding reached this point, Howie felt a peculiar stab at his own words. There was an echo of Paul's voice saying, "You never think."

It was not a small thing, his not thinking. He had led the twins into terrible danger.

There was a moment of silence. Then Dr. Stevens put one of his perfect cubes of steak in his mouth, chewed it, and smiled. The scolding was over.

"I suppose you are wondering why we are here," he said in a perfectly normal voice.

Howie and the twins looked at each other as if the thought had never entered their minds.

"We're from the James Medical School," said Dr. Stevens. "Tom and Bud are medical students, doing a special project with me on antibiotics. As for me, my field is dermatology—the study of the skin. That's why

I'm so interested in antibiotic medicines, such as penicillin, and the way they can be used in curing skin diseases and healing wounds."

Diane looked around the camp in bewilderment. "Why do you have to do research in a swamp?"

Howie and Joel were embarrassed. They thought Diane was being rude, but Dr. Stevens only laughed.

"I know it sounds silly to work in a swamp when we have a beautifully equipped laboratory back at the medical school. In fact, we don't actually do much research here. We're just collecting mud."

Howie and the twins stared at Dr. Stevens after this queer remark, but he quickly explained, "The state has long been interested in this swamp area. Land around here is too valuable to let a large tract just stand useless the way it is.

"The time has come for the swamplands to be used for something practical. There are industrial developers who want to drain the swamps and build factories here. That's a good idea, but some of us feel the swamplands can be used for medical purposes."

"How's that?" asked Howie.

"As you may know," said Dr. Stevens, "antibiotics are often extracted from soil. We have a hunch that the mud around here, which has been fermenting for years, may contain organic matter that would be an excellent source of antibiotics. If the boys and I can prove we're right, the state is willing to build a large medical research plant here for the study of antibiotics."

"You mean," said Howie, "that gook out there in the swamp could be used for healing people?"

"We don't know anything yet," sighed Dr. Stevens.

"Sometimes we go to a lot of trouble to study something, only to find we're barking up the wrong tree. That's research for you."

Joel was still eying the big tent with the radio antenna. "Is that your lab?" he asked curiously.

"Yes," said Tom. "Would it be all right for them to see the lab, Dr. Stevens?"

"Certainly," Dr. Stevens nodded. "Come along."

Pepper, roused from a dog-dream at the sound of Howie's leaving, started to follow expectantly. Dr. Stevens cast a sudden alarmed glance at the dog.

"Do you have a rope?" asked Howie. Visions of Pepper in a tent among glass test tubes floated before him. Tom found a rope and Pepper was tied firmly to a tree.

With Pepper wailing angrily outside, they entered the lab tent. It was a dim place, smelling of canvas and strange, sharp odors. Dr. Stevens turned on a light and a crude laboratory became evident, set up on planks supported by wooden sawhorses. Stands holding test tubes filled with muddy-looking liquid were lined up on the plank table. Behind them were odd-shaped beakers and retorts, a small electric stove, and an assortment of tightly stoppered bottles of chemicals.

"These are some of the mud samples we have taken from the swamp," Dr. Stevens explained to Howie and Diane.

Joel had wandered over to the other side of the tent to get a better look at the radio that fascinated him so much. Suddenly he yelled, "Hey, it's sputtering."

At first Howie and Diane didn't know what Joel was talking about, but Dr. Stevens calmly looked at his watch. "Time for the three-o'clock report," he said.

Bud went over to the radio and turned a knob. There was a small crackle and a voice said, "QX5R sending. BL12, do you hear me?"

"BL12 receiving. Hear you loud and clear," replied Bud.

"Hi, this is Joe," the voice on the radio said cheerily. "What's new at Operation Mudhole, Bud?"

"The radio is our communication with the college," Dr. Stevens said in a low voice. "It was rigged up for us by the medical electronics department."

Everyone clustered around the radio as Bud reported, "We put down some cores fifteen feet this morning. Haven't had a chance to see what we have yet."

Howie noticed two dirty-looking iron tubes. Those must be the "cores" that were sent to the bottom of the swamp to bring up mud.

"Bud, your mother called," said Joe on the radio. "She wanted me to remind you to keep your feet dry."

Bud snorted, "That's my mother!"

"Tell him about the eggs," Dr. Stevens interrupted.

Howie listened curiously. He wondered if Dr. Stevens had found some rare fish eggs in the swamp.

But no, Bud simply informed the radio, "We're all out of eggs. Also bacon and bread. Can you have the stuff for us when Tom comes tomorrow?"

It was just a shopping list. Even scientists had to eat.

Tom grabbed the microphone. "Hey, Joe," he called, "do me a favor, will you? Call Lucy and tell her I'll be in tomorrow afternoon."

"Okay," said Joe. "Keep plugging. Over and out."

"Over and out," said Bud.

"Once a week one of us takes the motorboat back to

the school for supplies. Gives us a chance to have a good hot bath and see our friends," Tom told them.

"Is it far?" asked Diane.

"About fifty miles. Takes a few hours with that putt-putt boat, but it's worth it to get back to civilization for a little while."

"You mean, back to your girl friend," teased Bud.

"Are those the cores you took from the swamp?" asked Howie, pointing at the iron tubes.

"That's right," replied Dr. Stevens. "We push these iron tubes down into the water with a rod. They fill up with mud and we pull them up. Then we examine the mud to see what we have."

"What have you found?" asked Diane excitedly.

"Lots of things," said Dr. Stevens. "By themselves they don't mean much, but we keep careful records. We write everything down in our logbook. When we have finished our experiments, we'll be able to study our notes and see the whole picture of the type of mud there is in the swamp." He held up a black note-book. "This little logbook will tell whether this swamp will become an industrial park or a medical labora-tory."

Howie gazed at the battered little book with interest. He wished he knew what final answer would be written in it. Then he surprised himself by saying, "I just did a research paper."

"Really?" Dr. Stevens asked, his bushy eyebrows go-ing up with interest.

Howie felt silly. Now, why did that have to pop out? After all, why should Dr. Stevens want to know about a social studies paper? "It wasn't anything much," he

shrugged. "Just a report on the religions of India and Pakistan. It wasn't real research. I got my information from the public library."

"Of course it was real research," stated Dr. Stevens. "That's what research is—digging out facts and then putting them together to see what you've found. Even Columbus was doing research. He wanted to find out what was doing on the other side of the Atlantic Ocean."

Howie smiled. Dr. Stevens was really nice.

"If you're the curious type, maybe you'll be interested in exploring what's in this mess," said Dr. Stevens, reaching for a flask of dirty water. "We've been saving this mud for two weeks."

Howie and the twins craned their necks to see better. Dr. Stevens pulled out the stopper and looked into the flask. "Beautiful!" he beamed.

"Ugh," said Diane, sniffing.

Dr. Stevens had a funny idea of beauty. The mud in the flask looked as if it had all turned bad. A grayish mold had grown all over the top of it. It had a terrible smell.

"Isn't it spoiled?" asked Joel timidly.

"That's what we wanted," chuckled Tom. "The mold, or fungus, is made of tiny plants. They're real hungry stuff. When some kinds of mold are injected into the body of a sick person, they gobble up the nourishment needed by the bacteria that are making the person sick

Then the bacteria starve to death and the person gets well."

Howie eyed the mold warily. "How do you know this is the right kind of mold?"

"Spoken like a real scientist," approved Dr. Stevens. "We don't know. This mold might be all wrong . . . or it might be just the kind we need to make antibiotics. That's why we test it."

Diane had been looking at the mold with a mixture of distaste and fascination. Finally she said, "Do you mean that stuff could make me well if I were sick? I should think it would make me sicker."

"It certainly would," Dr. Stevens agreed. "This is just the crude stuff from which the antibiotic is manufactured. It takes plenty of refining and testing before it is ready for doctors to use."

While they were talking, Bud had brought over a bowl and some white filter paper. He stretched the paper over the bowl and poured the contents of the test tube on it. The water seeped through the paper, leaving gooey, moldy mud on top.

"Let's see what we have here," said Dr. Stevens, carefully placing the filter paper with its load of sediment on a shallow dish.

Tom opened the logbook to a page marked "Sample 51." The page was dated with the day and time the sample had been taken from the swamp and told the location in the swamp in which the core had gone down. Now Tom noted the present date and waited, pen in hand, to record Dr. Stevens' findings.

Dr. Stevens took a stick that looked like a tongue depressor and delicately scooped up some of the fungus from the top of the mud, his hands moving in the same speedy, precise way they had when he cut up the steak.

Bud brought over a strip of blue paper. "Litmus," he explained. "Test for acid."

Dr. Stevens smeared a little of the fungus on the paper. Parts of the paper turned light pink.

"Slightly acid," wrote Tom in the logbook.

Next Bud set up a test tube in a holder. Dr. Stevens slipped another sample of fungus in the test tube, and opened a small bottle of chemical.

"Say!" exclaimed Diane. "That's nail polish remover."

The boys started to shush her, but Dr. Stevens grinned. "Made of the same stuff as nail polish remover —acetone."

He poured some of the acetone into the test tube and shook it vigorously. The acetone became muddy as the mold seemed to melt into it.

"Soluble in acetone," wrote Tom in his logbook.

Bud brought over another test tube and another bottle of chemical. When he opened the bottle, Howie sniffed.

"I know," he said. "Gas stations."

"Right," said Dr. Stevens. "This stuff is petroleum ether. Let's see if our mold will dissolve in it."

Once again he shook up some mold with the chemical. But this time, after Dr. Stevens stopped shaking, the mold sank down to the bottom of the test tube, leaving the petroleum ether clear.

"Insoluble in petroleum ether," wrote Tom.

"Very good," said Dr. Stevens, nodding in satisfaction. "Penicillin is soluble in acetone and insoluble in petroleum ether."

"Does that mean this stuff is penicillin?" asked Howie.

"By no means," Dr. Stevens replied. "These are just two simple tests. Many more complicated tests will have to be made in a real laboratory to see if there's enough of the right kind of mold in this mud. But we're beginning to feel the swamp contains some good material." He motioned to Bud. "Let's take a look at those slides we made of sample number 49."

Bud opened a small wooden chest and brought out two slides labeled "49-A" and "49-B." Both slides looked exactly alike, with a dirty smear in the center covered by a thin glass cover. But Dr. Stevens explained that to one slide some mold had been added, but not to the other.

Deftly he slipped "49-A" under the microscope. He looked through the eyepiece and said "Hmm." Then he put "49-B" under the microscope and said "Aha!"

The children were seething with suspense, wondering what Dr. Stevens had found out. Finally, he motioned with one finger to Howie to come over. Then he put slide "49-A" back. Howie peered into the eyepiece.

"What do you see?" asked Dr. Stevens.

"Little wormy things," said Howie.

"Those are bacteria," said Dr. Stevens. It gave Howie a queer little thrill to be actually looking at bacteria.

Diane and Joel crowded over to have a look too.

Then Dr. Stevens inserted the other slide. Howie took a look. This one was less interesting. There were no wormy things.

"Nothing there," he said, disappointed.

At that Tom and Bud became very excited. They came over and looked into the microscope.

"Well, I'll be darned," said Tom. "Maybe we have something."

"The mold killed the bacteria," said Dr. Stevens triumphantly. "Now all we need is about a hundred more finds like this and maybe we'll get our laboratory!"

"Boy!" exclaimed Howie. "That's terrific!"

But then his brow wrinkled. Something was bothering him. "The thing that worries me," he said slowly, "is how do they know that the mold itself won't harm people?"

"They don't know," said Dr. Stevens thoughtfully. "Work with antibiotics is a constant fight. For example, some people are allergic to penicillin. It makes them very sick. Then, some disease bacteria can build up such a resistance to the antibiotic, it doesn't work with them for long. There are still some diseases that are not affected by antibiotics at all. Who knows, maybe in this very swamp we might find a strain of mold that will do things the antibiotics we have now can't do."

Howie looked around the tiny tent laboratory. There, with bits of mud from a swamp, some funny-smelling chemicals, a microscope, and carefully kept records, was a small part of the battle scientists were fighting against disease. He began to have a very strong feeling that he must come back again and learn more about Dr. Stevens' work.

The silence in the tent was broken by loud howls coming from outside.

"Sounds like your dog is having a nervous breakdown," said Tom.

"He doesn't like to be tied up," said Howie. "I'd better go to him."

Pepper was straining against the rope, yipping his lungs out. When he saw Howie, he started dancing indignantly around his master.

"You're a pain in the neck," said Howie, untying him.

Pepper wagged his tail happily, as if Howie were saying he was the nicest dog in the world.

Dr. Stevens looked at Pepper fondly. "He reminds me of a beagle I once had named Sparky. Good hunting dog, that Sparky. When my son Jonathan was a teenager we used to go up to the mountains every fall for some hunting."

"What happened to Jonathan?" asked Diane.

"Oh," sighed Dr. Stevens in a voice he tried to make sound sad but was really bursting with pride. "He didn't come to much good. He's a heart surgeon in San Francisco."

"Dr. Jonathan Stevens promises to be one of the leading heart men in the country, but just because he doesn't tinker with test tubes his father doesn't think he's a scientist," said Tom.

"Oh, I don't know," teased Dr. Stevens. "They all have their places, even the cut-and-sew boys like Jonathan."

He looked over toward the west where the sun was just edging the top of the cypress tree. "Time you kids started for home," he said briskly. "You don't want to be going through this swamp area in the dark."

Howie smiled to himself. You could tell Dr. Stevens was a father. Once people were parents, they never seemed to get over it.

"Bud, suppose you tie the raft onto the motorboat and lead them out of the swamp," suggested Dr. Stevens.

"Sure thing," said Bud. "Come on, kids."

Diane and Joel started to follow Bud toward the motorboat, but Howie felt rooted to the spot. He looked over toward the lab tent longingly. Then he said timidly to Dr. Stevens, "Sir, would it bother you very much if the twins and I came to see you again?"

Hearing Howie's words, Diane came darting over to Dr. Stevens. "Oh, please let us," she begged, a dark flush of excitement rising in her face. "We can help you." She looked around at the greasy barbecue tools. "We can do dishes. And I know how to wash socks."

"You're in!" exclaimed Tom. "This camp surely needs a reliable girl who can wash dishes and socks."

But Dr. Stevens wasn't so enthusiastic.

"We certainly could use three such bright youngsters to help with the chores around here," he said. "It would give us more time for our work. But I'm afraid if I let you come, the whole town will want to come and watch us work. We've been keeping our operation here rather secret, not because we're unfriendly, but because we just can't be interrupted by sightseers."

"Oh, we'll keep it a secret. We won't tell a soul," Howie and Joel said quickly.

Dr. Stevens' eyebrows knitted themselves together thoughtfully like a pair of friendly caterpillars. Finally he said, "You would have to get the written permission of your parents. I would not like the responsibility of having you come to the swamp without their approval."

"Yes, yes," chorused Howie and the twins.

"Wait here," said Dr. Stevens, and disappeared into

the tent. He came out a few minutes later carrying two sheets of paper.

"I have notes here for your parents," he said, "explaining who we are. If they approve your coming, have them sign the notes on the bottom and bring them back to me."

As the children started to follow Bud, Dr. Stevens reminded them, "Remember, you're coming here as volunteer workers, not guests. You'll follow orders, just as Tom and Bud do, and I don't want any arguing over jobs. Understand?"

As the three nodded their heads vigorously, Dr. Stevens smiled. "Well, I hope we see you again soon. Bud, make sure you show them landmarks so they can find their way back again." He reached over and patted Pepper on the head. "Don't forget to bring 'man's best friend' back with you. We need a mascot."

7: The Promise

When Howie reached home, his mother greeted him at the door with a strange expression on her face. She seemed lit up, like a Hallowe'en pumpkin, with a happy secret. She was about to speak to him when she smelled something burning. "E-e-ek, the stew!" she cried, and rushed off to the kitchen.

Howie figured he just imagined his mother having a secret. He heard his father's car crunch on the driveway and ran out to greet him with a big smile. "Hi, Dad. How did things go at the plant today?"

Mr. Blake looked at him suspiciously. It wasn't like Howie to give him such a joyful greeting. "You in some kind of trouble?" he asked.

Howie put on his hurt expression that said, "You are

so unfair to me," although he knew his father spoke from experience.

"Of course not," he said. "But there is something important I want to talk to you about."

"Okay, okay," said Mr. Blake, putting away his coat. "Let's have it. If you've already used up your allowance, the answer is 'no.' "

Howie had used up his allowance buying equipment for the raft, but he said, "Oh, no, Dad, nothing like that."

He showed his father Dr. Stevens' note. Mr. Blake's expression changed, chameleonlike, from shock to anger to grim sorrow.

"So you went to the swamp area," he despaired. "I thought we could trust you. You're past twelve—do I have to keep a leash on you like Pepper?"

Howie hung his head. "I'm sorry, Dad," he said automatically.

"You're sorry!" roared Mr. Blake. "Didn't you realize the danger of such a venture? Don't you ever think?"

Howie shrugged uncomfortably.

Then his father softened a little. "How did you get there?"

"We built a raft," Howie said eagerly. "It's a real good raft—hardly leaks at all." He noticed a look of interest in his father's eyes and decided to take advantage of what he thought was a weakening by plunging ahead. "May I go back to the camp, Dad? Dr. Stevens says we can be volunteer workers."

But Mr. Blake was not weakening. He was still angry. "Certainly not," he said shortly. "I'll have to talk to your mother about this."

Mrs. Blake's hair was all in little curls from the heat of the stew pot and her face was pink. It seemed to Howie that the pinkness was not only from heat; it was part of that lit-up look he thought he had seen before.

She kissed her husband affectionately and started to say something, but he interrupted at once to tell her about the swamp.

All the pinkness disappeared from Mrs. Blake's face. She turned white. "You didn't!" she exclaimed to Howie. "Why, you could have been lost, or even drowned!"

Mr. Blake showed her the note. Her reaction was swift. "Out of the question. You are not to go back to that place."

"But Mom, we wouldn't get lost. Bud showed us landmarks and we know just how to find the camp," Howie pleaded.

"What's going on here?" Paul came sauntering into the kitchen. He sniffed at the stew. "It's burned."

"I know," said Mrs. Blake ruefully.

"What's the big excitement?"

"Howie and his friends built a raft and went into the swamp. They met some scientists or something, a Dr. Stevens. Now he wants permission to go back there and work with them." His mother handed Paul the note.

Paul read it and let out a long whistle. "Say, is he a dermatologist?"

"Yes," said Howie, surprised that Paul would know.

"Wow, what a break!" exclaimed Paul. "Our chemistry teacher was telling us about him—Dr. Arthur Stevens. He's one of the most famous men in his field in the country! He works on antibiotic medicines. In fact, our teacher told us he's been working on an important medicine called Stevens' Ointment, to help in the treatment of large wounds and surgical incisions."

Mr. and Mrs. Blake stopped looking angry and gazed at Paul in astonishment. Then Mrs. Blake said thoughtfully, "This sounds like the kind of thing Mr. Frost had in mind."

"Mr. Frost?" said her husband. "What does he have to do with this?"

Mrs. Blake's face dimpled into a smile and the lit-up look came back. She put an arm around Howie's shoulder for a moment. "Mr. Frost called me this morning. He told me Howie had done a remarkable job on a social studies paper. He's even recommending him for the advanced classes at the junior high school next year."

"You don't say!" exclaimed Mr. Blake. He smiled at Howie. "That's mighty good news, son. But I still don't see what it has to do with going to the swamp."

"Well," explained Mrs. Blake, "Mr. Frost said Howie needed to do harder jobs that would make him think. It seems to me that working with a famous scientist would be a good opportunity."

"I'll say! exploded Paul. "Imagine working with Dr. Arthur Stevens!"

Mr. Blake chewed his lower lip thoughtfully. Then he said to Howie, "Can I trust you not to do something dumb again, like taking your raft into dangerous places?"

"Of course," said Howie eagerly.

His father considered further. Finally he said, "All right, I'll let you go if the Matsons permit the twins to go."

"Whoopee!" shouted Howie, running to the telephone. "I'll dial their number for you, Dad."

Convincing Mr. and Mrs. Matson was not so simple.
They had been as horrified as Mr. Blake that their children had gone to the swamp. When the Blakes called,
the Matson twins had just received an emphatic "No!"
to their plea to go back to the swamp. It took the
combined efforts of Mr. and Mrs. Blake and Paul explaining about Dr. Stevens to persuade the Matsons to
change their minds, but at last the twins received their
permission.

The *Diane* made her second trip to the swamp the
next Saturday, and it was very different from the first
one. Following the landmarks Bud had showed them,
the children went directly to the camp. It was amazing
how easy it was to find once you knew how.

Dr. Stevens and his assistants greeted them warmly
and soon found plenty of odd jobs that needed doing
around the camp. There were dishes to wash, trash to
burn, and tidying up around the lab. As she had promised, Diane washed socks. When she went into the sleeping tent to fetch them, she noticed rumpled cots. She
made them up with crisp hospital corners, just as she
had learned in Girl Scout camp.

"Whew, just like home," said Tom admiringly when
he saw Diane's perfect work.

"Not like my home," scoffed Joel. "My mother would
faint if she saw this."

Dr. Stevens didn't say much, but he seemed very
pleased at the quick and willing attitude the children
took toward their work. They didn't realize he was actually testing them until he said quite casually on the

second Saturday, "Come on into the lab tent. I've got some work for you to do there."

First he asked them to sterilize some test tubes. Then he showed them how to use the microscope. Then, to their excited delight, he let them make some slides of specimens.

More often than not, their clumsy fingers bungled the delicate work. There were times when they would try to get the specimens under the little cover glasses and end up with the specimens at one end and the cover glass at the other.

But Dr. Stevens never scolded. His quick fingers would fix the specimen in one deft movement and he'd say, "Don't worry. This takes lots of experience."

By the end of the afternoon, the children were beginning to get the hang of the work. Dr. Stevens proudly called them "my junior apprentices." They could hardly wait to come back the third Saturday and do more lab work.

It was on the morning of the third Saturday that Dr. Stevens and Howie made their secret, unspoken pact.

Bud had gone to the medical college for supplies, so Dr. Stevens and Tom were alone in the camp. Tom came into the lab tent as Dr. Stevens was starting the children off on some new specimens.

"I'm ready to go and sink those cores now," said Tom.

"Oh," said Dr. Stevens, "I'm afraid I can't go with you —I'm right in the middle of an experiment."

Tom looked a little puzzled. "Someone has to take care of the log," he said. "Bud's not here."

Dr. Stevens reached up to the shelf and took down the little black book. "Howie, how about you doing the log?"

As the doctor put the little book in his hands, Howie felt a tingle go up his spine. Dr. Stevens looked at him very intently and said, "Take good care of it."

Howie stood silently for a moment, holding the book. Although nothing more was said, he sensed that Dr. Stevens knew how much the lab work meant to him.

As he felt the worn leather in his hands, Howie had the feeling he was making a promise. It was a strange kind of promise, for he was free to break it. It was the pledge to do the same kind of work when he became a man that Dr. Stevens was doing—to look for ways to heal people.

The world was so full of interesting kinds of work, Howie did not have to choose this one way now, and never change his mind. But there was one part of the promise he knew he would never break once he made it. That was what Dr. Stevens meant when he said "Take care of it." He wanted Howie to promise to undertake all responsibilities as he was accepting the log book now —to treat them with very great care.

He looked at the book, and then at Dr. Stevens.

"Yes, sir," he said. The promise had been made. It would never be broken.

Tom and Howie got into the motorboat, and it putt-putted softly between the banks of the little river. Willows arched greenly overhead. On the banks of the stream the leaves of the swamp laurel glistened in the sun and here and there were the little pink bells of the leatherleaf flower. It was hard to believe that just beyond lay Deadwood Lake, as they had named the drowned forest.

"How is it that Bud didn't take the boat to the college?" Howie asked.

"We need it to sink cores, so he took the train from Sumner," Tom replied.

After that the two lapsed into silence. Howie guessed that Tom must be thinking of Lucy, to whom he was engaged. He was just as glad. He had some thinking of his own to do.

He was remembering a story Dr. Stevens had told the Saturday before, when they were all sitting around the campfire after lunch.

"I was in the South Pacific during World War Two," said Dr. Stevens. "My job was to examine civilians to see if they had leprosy. Can you imagine—here I was, a dermatologist with years of experience treating diseases of the skin, yet sometimes I had trouble recognizing it."

Dr. Stevens tapped his pipe on a rock and his usually calm voice became excited. "We have no idea, in our safe, sanitary United States, of some of the diseases that afflict people in many parts of the world. And all because there aren't enough scientists with the knowledge to help them."

He stared at the fire and said, "It was at that moment, there in the South Pacific, that I decided I was going into research so I could help rid the world of some of its ills."

Howie wasn't even aware that he was staring at Dr. Stevens as if hypnotized until he noticed the doctor looking at him curiously. Then he shook his head and grinned with embarrassment.

But the memory of what Dr. Stevens had said had remained with him all week. It became linked up with what he was studying in school. The meaning of all that reading and studying about countries in Africa and Asia wasn't just boundaries and the names of capital cities.

It was about people. Many of them were poor. Some of them were sick. They needed help.

As the motorboat turned into Deadwood Lake, Howie clutched the little log book tighter. It was funny, but just keeping a neat record in a black leather book could be very important.

Tom anchored the boat in the middle of the lake. "Ready?" he grinned at Howie. "Just listen to everything I say and write it down clearly."

He took out a compass. "Forty-seven point two east."

Howie wrote the date on a clean page and carefully took down Tom's words.

Several times they changed their location and Tom sank new cores, each time dictating data to Howie. The information on the page grew into a neat record of depths and places.

Tom wiped off the cores and stored them in the bottom of the boat. He looked at the sun, which had reached a mid-point in the sky. "Something tells me it's time for lunch."

Howie didn't need the sun to tell him that. His stomach was just as reliable.

They cruised across the lake, skillfully avoiding submerged logs and rocks. By now Deadwood Lake was as familiar to Howie as the streets of Thorneywoods. It was no longer frightening, but the silence of the place was still eerie. He was glad when they turned back toward the live forest and the island.

8: Pepper

Howie and Tom tied up the boat and waded ashore, carrying the cores. Howie made sure the log book was safe and dry in his pocket.

"Hey," shouted Tom, "what do I smell? The exotic fragrances of the Orient?"

"Chicken!" exclaimed Howie.

The two scrambled up the bank toward the tantalizing aroma. As they approached the camp, Pepper came yipping through the bushes to greet them. As the dog did his usual circle dance around him, Howie stopped and patted his head.

"You old phony," he smiled. He knew, in spite of Pepper's air of having endured an unbearable separation, that he had been living in a dog heaven between Dr.

Stevens' spoiling and the endlessly fascinating smells of the woods.

They came upon Dr. Stevens standing over a large stew pot on the kerosene stove, with a towel tied around his waist for an apron. His face was as rosy as an apple from the heat. Joel and Diane, also looking rosy, hovered with him over the pot. It was clear from the chickeny, oniony fragrance that they had been concocting a masterpiece. Dr. Stevens saluted Tom and Howie with a wooden spoon. "Welcome," he said, making a deep bow, "to the Stevens Swampside Elite Restaurant, featuring homemade chicken stew created by the famous chef, Arthur Stevens, and those incomparable cooks, the Matson twins."

With great ceremony he lifted the lid off the pot. A white cloud of steam rose up, revealing fluffy dumplings nestled on top of chicken swimming in golden gravy.

"Oh, boy!" said Howie.

"Hurry and wash up," said Diane. "We're starved. We've been waiting for you for hours."

Howie and Tom ran to get the mud off their hands. Then they all sat down on a ring of stones they had placed around the campfire.

"This looks like a Druids' circle," Dr. Stevens commented as he ladled out portions of chicken.

"What's a Druid?" asked Joel.

"Ancient Britons," said Tom. "They used to worship stones. They painted themselves blue."

"You're fooling!" Diane exclaimed.

"Nope. Honest Injun. They did. May I have some more chicken, Dr. Stevens?"

Dr. Stevens scraped the last of the chicken out of the pot. "If anyone ever has problems with leftovers, I'd tell him to go camping with a twenty-two-year-old medical student, two twelve-year-old boys and a twelve-year-old girl."

"And one dog," added Howie.

Pepper was snoozing peacefully, looking fat and satisfied. Even he had had enough chicken. Suddenly his ears cocked. A small gray shape whisked through the trees and the dog shot out after it.

"Pepper feels it's his duty to rid the woods of rabbits," laughed Dr. Stevens.

"Don't worry," commented Tom, "the rabbits have formed an anti-Pepper association. He's not going to catch one so fast."

"Say," said Dr. Stevens, "I've got something to show you kids. Tom brought it back from the college last week."

He went into the lab tent and came back carrying a small white jar. He unscrewed the top and showed the children what looked like yellow cold cream.

Howie's eyes sparkled. "I know what that is! It's Stevens' Ointment."

"How did you know?" asked Dr. Stevens, surprised.

Howie told him about Paul's chemistry teacher.

Dr. Stevens shook his head. "I'm afraid your brother's teacher is a bit optimistic. Stevens' Ointment is far from perfected yet. This is just a sample the lab made up from a new formula I worked out before I came here."

The twins looked at the little jar. Diane wrinkled her nose. "It smells funny."

"What's it good for?" asked Joel.

"It's going to heal large wounds and help in major surgery," Howie quoted Paul.

Joel eyed the jar with interest. "Say," he said, starting to unpeel a bandage strip from his finger, "I broke a glass and cut myself yesterday. Maybe your ointment will be good for my cut."

"No," said Dr. Stevens a little sharply. "Don't put that on your finger. This formula hasn't been tested yet." He sighed. "If it turns out like all the others have for the past ten years, it isn't safe for man or beast."

"Do you mean it took you ten years to make this medicine?" Diane exclaimed.

"That's nothing in research chemistry," said Dr. Stevens. "Forty years passed from the time Pasteur first noticed the penicillin mold until Dr. Fleming perfected it."

Diane shook her head. "Won't you feel terrible if it's no good after it took you so long to make it?"

Dr. Stevens shrugged. "It won't be the first time I thought I had the formula and was mistaken. I'll just have to start all over again."

He replaced the cap on the jar. "When we finish this swamp project and go back to the college, we'll start testing the ointment again, trying it out on a lot of animals to see if it's safe. Who knows? Maybe this time I've got it right."

He peered over his glasses at Howie. "Please get the log book. Let's see how it's going."

As he went to get the book, Howie once again had the feeling that Dr. Stevens was giving him a message. There was a connection between the story of Stevens'

Ointment and the log book. Dr. Stevens wanted to be sure Howie understood that scientific research was not all excitement. It was often just disappointing hard work.

Dr. Stevens looked over the log book and smiled approvingly. "Very nice work. Everything is systematic and clear."

His blue eyes looked solemnly at Howie. "Would you like to continue doing the log?"

Howie thought fleetingly of the ten years Dr. Stevens had spent working on his ointment. It wasn't only the log Dr. Stevens was asking about.

Then he remembered the people all over the world

who were waiting for scientists to find new ways to cure disease.

He looked straight at the doctor. "Yes," he said firmly, "I should like it very much."

Dr. Stevens smiled. "Fine, then. The log is yours while you're in camp. Now, let's see if you and Joel can do as neat and thorough a job on the dishes as you did on the log."

"What about me?" asked Diane.

"For you, young lady," said Dr. Stevens, pretending to tweak her nose, "I've got a bag of dirty socks and some laundry soap. Please take them down to the river and get them nice and clean."

Dr. Stevens and Tom disappeared into the lab tent to work and Diane went swinging down the hill toward the river carrying a bag of dirty socks and humming, "This is the way we wash our clothes. . . ."

"And to think my mother can't even get her to pick her socks off the floor, much less wash them!" Joel shook his head.

Howie circled warily around the greasy stew pot. "Ugh," he said.

Joel poked around in the pot with a spoon. "Well, that was the bargain. We said we'd do chores. We might as well get at it."

"Hardly pays to eat when you have a dirty pot like this," Howie grumbled. "Here, scoop up some of that stuff on the bottom onto this paper. Pepper'll eat it."

He took the paper with its load of scraps over to the edge of the woods and called, "Here, Pepper. Come eat." Then he went back to Joel.

They scraped at the pot and rubbed it with sand and poured water on it. Then Joel said, "Let's take it down to the river. It'll be easier to rinse there."

"Okay," Howie replied.

On the way to the river they passed the food Howie had set out for Pepper. It had not been touched.

"That's funny," said Howie. "Pepper always comes when he hears the word 'eat.' "

"Do you suppose he got lost chasing that rabbit?" asked Joel.

"Impossible," said Howie. "This is a small island and Pepper knows every inch of it."

Diane was squatting at the edge of the river pounding the wet socks on a flat rock.

"What do you think you're doing?" asked her brother.

"Didn't your class see that film strip, 'Primitive Laundry Methods in India'?"

"Those socks will be more than primitive if you keep that up. They'll be full of holes," scoffed her brother.

Diane held up a sock and eyed it critically. "Maybe you're right. I could pound too much. This look clean enough?"

"Spotless," said Howie, dunking the pot in the river. "Have you seen Pepper?"

"No. Why? Hey, get out of here. You're making the water all dirty. You'll get garbage all over my clean socks."

Howie hastily moved the pot a safe distance away. "It's funny—Pepper didn't come when I left food for him."

"If I know Pepper," said Diane, wringing out a pair of

white sweat socks, "he's up there bothering Dr. Stevens. And it's Dr. Stevens' own fault. He shouldn't be so kind to him."

Restlessly, Howie handed the pot over to Joel. "I'd better go up to the lab tent then. I don't want the dog to get in their way."

He sprinted up the hill, more anxious to reassure himself that Pepper was safe than to keep the dog from bothering Dr. Stevens.

Dr. Stevens and Tom were squinting at some slides under the microscope.

"Have you seen Pepper?" asked Howie.

They looked up and blinked a little at the interruption. "No, he hasn't been around here."

"Oh," said Howie.

He was beginning to get alarmed. Seeing Joel and Diane coming up the hill, he ran over to them.

"Dr. Stevens and Tom haven't seen Pepper either," he called. "I'm going to look for him."

"Wait," called Diane, hanging the wet clothes on a clothesline. "I'll come with you."

"Me too," said Joel. "Just let me put the pot away."

"And get the machete, while you're at it," Howie said.

Howie and the twins searched along the paths in the woods, whistling and calling. Then they left the path and started to beat their way through the dense underbrush. They could hear the flutter of wings and small scamperings as the wood creatures fled at their approach. But there was no sign of Pepper.

They pushed on until they came to the empty beach on the other side of the island.

"Do you think he could have gone into the water and drowned?" asked Howie frantically.

"Not Pepper," comforted Joel. "Remember how he swam after the boat? He doesn't drown easily."

"What'll we do?" Howie implored. He was so worried by this time, he couldn't think.

"Let's walk down the beach to the tip of the island and go through the woods that way," suggested Diane.

The woods were even thicker and more brambly coming from that direction, but the three hacked their way forward, calling "Pepper. Here, boy." The only answer was the urgent caw of a bird high overhead in a cypress tree.

"Pepper, please answer," called Howie. "Here boy, *here* boy!"

Suddenly Joel put up his hand. "Listen," he whispered.

Howie and Diane listened. From the other side of a big maple they heard a little whine. Howie started running toward the sound, not caring how scratched he got. A twig whipped against his face, cutting his cheek, but he didn't stop.

Then he took a step but his foot didn't hit the ground. It kept on going down, down. He felt Joel grab his arm and tug him back.

The boys and Diane looked down at a pit covered with old leaves and branches. The center of it was moving. They could hear a muffled whimpering.

Howie made his way down into the pit and tore away the leaves. There lay Pepper, one leg caught tightly in the jaws of a rusty iron trap. Blood seeped from an ugly cut on his side. When the dog saw Howie he stopped whimpering and weakly wagged his tail.

"Oh, Pepper, Pepper," cried Howie, kneeling down and trying to remove the trap.

Joel and Diane reached down and helped Howie pull at it.

"Must have been left here by a hunter," Joel panted.

"Careful," sobbed Howie. "He's hurt enough already."

They pulled on the trap as gently as they could. Finally the old rusty spring creaked open.

Howie picked Pepper up in his arms. Blood ran all over his clothes, but he didn't notice. The dog lifted his head a little and tried to lick Howie's face. Then he closed his eyes and let his head rest on Howie's shoulder.

Joel and Diane went ahead and cut a path through the bushes while Howie followed. Pepper wasn't a big dog, but after a while Howie's arms ached from carrying him. It seemed as though they would never get back to the camp.

At last they reached the clearing, and Howie laid the dog down near the campfire. Diane, not knowing what else to do, make a little pillow out of leaves and grass to go under the dog's head, while Joel ran for help.

Dr. Stevens and Tom rushed out of the lab tent. The doctor knelt down next to the dog and examined the wound with those swiftly moving fingers of his. He shook his head. "A mean wound." Then he brushed the blood-matted fur gently with one finger. "Rust," he said. "How did this happen?"

"He was caught in an old trap," said Howie miserably. "Is he going to die?" His throat was all tight.

"Not if we can help it," said Dr. Stevens shortly.

Then he began to call out orders. "Boiling water. Towels. My instrument bag."

Tom ran and put a kettle of water on the kerosene stove. Meanwhile Diane ran to the tent for clean towels and Joel rushed to find Dr. Stevens' instrument bag.

"Bring a razor, too," Dr. Stevens called after Joel.

When everything was ready, Dr. Stevens dipped a towel in the boiling water and swabbed away as much blood as he could. Then he sterilized the razor in the boiling water and shaved away the hair around the cut.

"I'm going to have to stitch this up," he said, "and I have no anesthetic. You boys will have to hold him down."

Howie took hold of Pepper's head and Joel held his front paws. Diane reached to help too, but Dr. Stevens held up his hand.

"I need you as a surgical nurse," he said. "Now, you just listen to everything I tell you and do what I say quickly, without asking questions. We have to hurry—he's losing too much blood."

He reached into his bag and took out a pair of surgical gloves and plunged them into the boiling water. Before slipping on the gloves he handed Diane a long surgical needle.

"Sterilize it," he ordered.

Diane sterilized the needle and handed it to Dr. Stevens, who quickly threaded it from a roll of surgical thread he had taken from the bag. "Good thing I have this emergency equipment," he grunted. "I figured you never can tell what can happen out in the woods."

He raised the needle, looked at the boys, and said, "Ready!"

As the needle went into the dog's skin, Pepper uttered a sharp "Yipe" and squirmed.

"Hold him," ordered Dr. Stevens. Howie and Joel took a firmer grip.

Dr. Stevens tried to pull the slippery sides of the wound together. "Wish I had some clamps," he said, perspiring.

Tom bent down and held the wound closed while Dr. Stevens' needle flashed in and out of the dog's skin. Every so often he would say "Wipe" to Diane, and she would wipe away as much blood as she could with the towel.

Howie kept saying, "It's all right, Pepper. It's all right," although he didn't know if it was all right at all.

At last Dr. Stevens cut the thread. His eyebrows drew together as he inspected his work.

"Ought to heal if we keep him quiet," he said. "The big danger is infection. Rust can be a nasty business."

As he straightened up he said, "It's a good thing I have some penicillin here. Brought it along in case one of us caught the flu or something. I'll give him a good shot and maybe that'll control the infection."

He found a hypodermic needle in the bag and started to sterilize it, saying, "Howie, go to the lab tent and find the penicillin. It's in a little bottle on the top shelf."

Howie ran to the tent and rummaged around the top shelf until he found the little bottle. He grabbed it and ran over to Dr. Stevens.

Dr. Stevens reached out for the bottle. Howie was in such a hurry to have him use it that he pulled out the stopper before giving it to him. As he started to hand it over he was so nervous that he knocked his hand against the hypodermic needle.

"Ow," he exclaimed as he felt the sharp prick.

Then he looked in horror at the penicillin bottle. He had tipped it over. The penicillin was running over the ground in a tiny stream.

Everyone just stared at the empty bottle.

"I don't have any more of that," said Dr. Stevens harshly. "Why did you open the bottle?"

Tears ran down Howie's cheeks. "I . . . I didn't think," he whispered.

The words echoed hollowly in his ears. His old excuse didn't mean much now. That bottle of penicillin could mean Pepper's life.

Seeing Howie's distress, Dr. Stevens' voice became gentler. "I know. You were just trying to make it easier for me. You didn't mean it, Howie."

He turned toward the dog, stared at the wound, and shook his head. "Nothing left to do but bandage him up and pray," he said. "He's lost too much blood to try to get him back to town."

"What about the Stevens' Ointment, sir? That's an antibiotic," said Tom.

Dr. Stevens pursed his lips. "Yes, *if* the Stevens' Ointment works, it would be a good thing to use. But this formula hasn't ever been tried—it might damage the dog more than it would help him."

"What will happen if you don't use it?" asked Howie.

"There's a grave chance that infection will set in.

After all the loss of blood this animal has had, I don't know whether he has the strength to fight off infection."

"Then he'll die!" cried Howie. "Dr. Stevens, please try the ointment!"

"Howie, are you willing to allow your dog to be used for experimental purposes?" asked Dr. Stevens. "If we are successful it will help prove that Stevens' Ointment can be used safely on people. But we might fail."

Howie gulped. "Dr. Stevens, please take the chance. I know your ointment will make Pepper better."

"Very well," Dr. Stevens sighed. "I hope you're right, Howie. I hope you're right."

Tom got the jar of ointment and a roll of bandage. Dr. Stevens took a wooden tongue depressor from a box in his bag and smeared the ointment thickly over the wound. Then he bandaged Pepper around his belly and his leg.

"You'll have to leave him here," he said. "He could never make that trip home on the raft."

Howie and Diane made Pepper a soft bed, using a paper carton and some rags. Then Dr. Stevens laid the dog gently in the carton. Pepper whined softly and looked at Howie. He seemed to know Howie was leaving him.

Howie reached over to the spot at the back of Pepper's head where he always liked to be rubbed. "You be good, Pepper," he said. "I'll be back to get you next week."

Then he and the twins sadly walked down the path leading to the place where the *Diane* was beached. Silently they shoved the raft into the water and started down the river toward Deadwood Lake and home.

Howie dipped his paddle listlessly in and out of the still waters of the lake. The lifeless trees matched his mood.

"Don't worry, Howie," said Diane. "Tom and Dr. Stevens said they'd take turns watching Pepper. If anything should go wrong, they'd notice it right away."

"Diane's right," Joel agreed. "Besides, don't forget, Dr. Stevens is a famous doctor."

Howie pushed angrily on his paddle. "It's all my fault. Why did I have to spill the penicillin?"

"It could have happened to anyone," Joel said consolingly.

"No, it couldn't," said Howie stubbornly. "Things like that are always happening only to me. Why am I that way, Joel? Why do I always do things without thinking?"

Joel had no answer to that. He paddled silently a while and then he said, "You mustn't forget Dr. Stevens' ointment. He's worked on it for ten years—it must be good. And just think, Dr. Stevens is using Pepper to experiment on. That makes Pepper a hero."

"I don't want my dog to be a dead hero." Tears rolled down Howie's cheeks. "I want him to be a live dog."

The worst thing Howie had to bear that week was not being able to find out what was happening with Pepper. How he wished Dr. Stevens had a telephone! But there was no way of getting in touch with the camp.

As the days dragged on, Howie began to dread going to the swamp on Saturday. He knew he would get more and more nervous as the raft drew near the camp, worrying about what news he would learn when he arrived there.

Then suddenly on Thursday night the telephone rang.

"James Medical College?" asked Mr. Blake, surprised. "Are you sure you have the right number? You say you want to speak to Howard Blake?"

Hearing the conversation, Howie rushed out to the hall and fairly snatched the telephone from his father's hand. "Hello, hello," he said nervously, "this is Howie Blake."

A man's voice answered. "This is Dr. Mansfield. I have a message for you from Dr. Stevens. He radioed it in from the camp and asked me to call you. He says your dog is all right. He's healing up fine."

Howie's voice went dry. "Thanks," he said faintly. Then, "Are you sure?"

"Oh, yes," said Dr. Mansfield. "That ointment certainly did a remarkable job. Your dog may be famous. He may even be written up in a medical journal."

Then Howie realized that this meant more to Dr. Stevens than just healing Pepper. It meant that after ten years' work on the ointment he might finally be successful. "I'm so glad. I'm so glad," he said in a rush. "And thank you for calling me."

Mr. Blake took the telephone. "You say the dog is all right? It was mighty nice of you to call."

"Oh, don't mention it," said Dr. Mansfield. "Dr. Stevens knew the boy would be worried. He wanted to set his mind at ease."

As soon as his father put down the telephone, Howie ran around the house telling the good news to everyone. Soon the entire Blake family was in a hubbub, everyone wanting to know all the details.

"Imagine," said Paul, "our dog being the first person to be cured by Stevens' Ointment. Wait till I tell my chemistry teacher about this."

"Pepper isn't a person. He's an animal," his father corrected him dryly.

The rest of the family stared at Mr. Blake. Then they burst out laughing. It had never occurred to any of them that Pepper wasn't a person. Certainly no one had ever told Pepper about it.

9: Howie's Big Mistake

When Howie and the twins were a hundred feet away from the camp they heard Pepper barking. Howie never thought he'd feel that Pepper's stubborn yapping would sound like music, but it did now.

Then, as they came up the hill from the river, they heard Bud's voice yelling, "Hurry up, Howie. I can't keep this hound down much longer!"

Howie ran to the tent and found Bud trying to pin the dog down in his carton. "He sure knew you were coming," puffed the young man.

"Quiet, boy, you have to get better," soothed Howie.

"*He* has to get better!" said Bud indignantly. "Have you any idea what this pup put us through? As soon as he started to feel better all he wanted to do was to jump out of the box and chase rabbits again. And we had to make him stay put so his stitches wouldn't come out!"

"Gee, I'm sorry he caused you so much trouble," Howie started to apologize. But then he noticed that Bud was grinning.

"How about that!" said Bud. "Only a week ago that dog was half dead. Now look at him! Stevens' Ointment certainly fixed him up."

Dr. Stevens, Tom, and the twins came into the tent.

"Do you want to see how he's healing?" Dr. Stevens asked.

Howie nodded, and Dr. Stevens gently removed part of the bandage. Healthy pink skin covered the ugly wound. Howie and the twins gazed at Dr. Stevens in awe. "Gee, Dr. Stevens, I don't know how to thank you." Howie's voice was thick with emotion.

Dr. Stevens chuckled. "Curing one dog of a deep rusty wound does not prove a medicine," he said. "We have to do a lot more testing." He gave the dog an affectionate pat. "Pepper here did us a great service, though. He's going to be part of a report for a medical journal."

"I know," Howie said. "Dr. Mansfield told me when he called." He shook his head. "I sure was glad you radioed the college about Pepper. I never was so happy to get a telephone call in my life!"

As they left the tent, Howie asked if he could take Pepper home.

"Yes," said Dr. Stevens. "But be very careful not to jiggle him too much. How will you get him home from the river?"

"That's taken care of," Howie assured him. "My

mother told me to call her from the boathouse. She's coming with the car to get us."

"You did a nice neat job on the log book," Dr. Stevens commented. "Care to work on it some more?"

Howie wanted to say "Oh boy, you bet!" but he had the feeling that would not be dignified and scientific, so he just replied, "Yes, sir, that would be fine."

Dr. Stevens seated himself on a rock and took the black leather log book out of his pocket. The morning sun, risen above the tree tops, poured down its warmth.

"Hot for early June," said the doctor, wiping his brow.

Howie removed his sweater. It was hot.

"We brought our bathing suits. Is it all right for us to swim in the river?" Joel asked.

"Capital idea!" exclaimed Dr. Stevens. Then, as the twins looked uncertainly at Howie, Dr. Stevens asked, "Would you rather go swimming than work on the log book?"

"Oh, no, " replied Howie quickly. "I'll meet you at the river later," he said to Diane and Joel.

"Don't go out of hearing of the dinner bell," Dr. Stevens warned.

"We won't," said the twins, and scampered away to change into their bathing suits.

Dr. Stevens spread the log book out on the rock. Howie noticed that more material had been added to the notes he had taken the week before.

"We've accomplished a lot this week," said the doctor proudly. "The boys have been taking cores all week—so far, excellent specimens. I think we've hit a rich source of antibiotic material in this black, mucky swamp."

"Does this mean you'll build the research station here?" asked Howie.

Dr. Stevens thoughtfully cleaned his glasses. "Looks good," he said. "But you know, it takes money to build laboratories. The government needs proof before they'll grant us the money."

Howie started to squat down on the baking hot rock, then quickly jumped up again. "Burns my legs," he explained. "Sure is hot!"

Very gingerly he sat down, carefully putting his sweater under his bare legs to protect them from the hot stone. He glanced intently at the closely written pages of the book. He could make out the dates and some of the more common chemical terms, but there were a lot of strange mathematical symbols that were new to him.

"Will the government give you the money when they see the log book?"

"I'm hoping so," Dr. Stevens smiled. He tapped the book with his fingernail. "This little book might be worth at least a hundred thousand dollars."

He handed it over to Howie. The warm leather felt alive. One hundred thousand dollars! Howie touched it as if it were studded with diamonds. Dr. Stevens laughed. "Just be careful of it, that's all. Now, run over to the lab tent. Bud could use your help."

The lab tent was stifling. It seemed as if the smell of canvas had detached itself from the tent and had settled in layers all about them. The odor of the chemicals and mud didn't help much either. Insects buzzed around the light bulb.

Bud sat at the table, stripped to the waist, sorting

little scraps of paper. "Whew!" he said to Howie. "It's a good thing we're finishing up our work here. This island must be some hole in the summer."

"If they build the research station, will it be too hot to work here during the summer?" asked Howie.

Bud laughed. "You won't know this place when they get through building," he said. "They'll bring in bulldozers to cut down the underbrush and big fogging machines to kill the insects. Then they'll build a nice concrete building, all glass windows and stainless steel lab equipment and air conditioning."

"Air conditioning . . . yeah," murmured Howie, seeing in his mind's eye this glittering paradise. "All for a hundred thousand dollars."

He opened the log book and Bud handed him a pen. "Where'd you get that figure?" he asked.

"From Dr. Stevens. He said the log book could be worth at least a hundred thousand dollars if he gets the government grant."

"That it can," Bud grinned. Then he looked keenly at Howie. "You like money?"

The question startled Howie. There seemed to be a hidden meaning behind it. "Of course I like money," he said. "That is, I never thought about a lot of money— that's for things like labs. But I do like a little bit of money to buy things I want."

Bud looked pleased. "It's important, if you want to do research work, to have the right idea about money. As you said, money is for labs and things. There isn't much left over to pay scientists. If you want to be rich, stay out of this line of work."

Howie settled down in the folding chair, the log book

in his lap. In spite of the sweltering heat, he felt very, very happy. It was wonderful the way Bud was talking to him as if he were a grown man. He looked at the thin, rather angular face of the young student. There weren't too many years between them, after all. He was just going into his teens and Bud had just left them. Maybe someday they would work together.

"Come on," said Bud briskly. "Let's stop dreaming about air conditioning and get this work done before we melt into two puddles of grease."

He gathered up the scraps of paper and started to dictate the information scribbled on them.

"June third . . . core one hundred eighteen, depth five feet . . . content ten percent acetone, twenty-eight percent insoluble matter. . . ."

Howie couldn't help it, but he began to feel his scientific enthusiasm beginning to falter. Bud's droning voice seemed endless, and the lines and lines of numbers just followed one another in monotonous succession. His arms and back were coated with sweat. Every so often a buzzing insect would come darting around the back of his neck and bite him. Wearily he kept pushing the pen along. He gritted his teeth. He had to be neat—above all things, he had to be neat. The log book mustn't be messed up!

From outside he could hear the faint sounds of laughter and splashing. That would be Joel and Diane having their lovely swim. Howie could just imagine the delicious sparkle of the water and the cool shade of the trees.

Bud crumpled up the papers as he finished with them. Soon there were soggy little balls all over the table. The whole tent was soggy and crawly. Howie began to feel sick.

"Say, you don't look so well," said Bud. "Want to quit?"

Howie shrugged his shoulders. "If you can stand it, I can," he said.

"That's the spirit," grinned Bud. "Just a few more notes, and we'll be through."

At last Bud finished with all the scraps of paper. "That does it!" he exclaimed. He examined the log book and nodded his approval.

"Thanks a lot," he said. "Your help sure speeded things up for me. Now, you go take your swim. I'm going to have a shower and a little nap."

Howie started to put the log book down on the table.

"Uh, uh," said Bud, sweeping the little balls of paper into a trash box. "Don't leave the book here—this place is too messy. Give it to Dr. Stevens."

As Howie left the tent, a healing blast of cool air coming up from the river hit him. The cries of Joel and Diane enjoying their swim were almost too much to bear. He looked around for Dr. Stevens but couldn't find him. The motorboat was gone, so he must have gone to Deadwood Lake with Tom.

Tucking the log book into his back pocket, he went into the sleeping tent to check on Pepper. This was a mistake, he soon realized, for Pepper only wanted to climb out of the box and follow him. Howie rummaged around in the food supplies until he found a box of crackers. He scattered some in the dog's box, and while Pepper was busying chewing one cracker after another, he slipped out of the tent.

Bud came dashing out of the shower, shaking drop-
lets of water from his hair. "Hey," he yelled, "you'd
better get your swim in. Dr. Stevens and Tom will be
back any minute and they'll want to eat lunch."

Howie grabbed his swimming trunks and ran down
the hill.

The sound of a long scream, followed by laughter,
echoed from the brook. Howie peered through a curtain
of leaves at the water's edge, curious to see what was
going on. Joel and Diane were having a water fight.
They were so busy kicking and splashing, they didn't
see him.

As he ducked behind a bush to change into his trunks
he decided to give them a good surprise. Joel had his
back to him, a terrific target for a sudden splash of cold
water. Howie crept along behind the bushes until he
came to some stones at the edge of the water, right behind where Joel was standing. Giggling to himself, he
started for the water. Then he noticed that he was still
foolishly carrying his khaki shorts.

He dropped the shorts on a rock and sneaked into the
water, carefully avoiding splashing sounds. Diane noticed him and opened her mouth, but he signaled her to
be quiet. Dimpling with fun, she let out a yell to distract Joel's attention. He started after her, but before he
could take a step, Howie scooped up a handful of water
and plunged it over his friend's head. Joel roared with
surprise, then turned and started pelting Howie with
water in return. The water was icy against Howie's skin,
so he ducked for a fast wetting.

Taking slow, easy strokes, he swam away from his
friends. Then he lay on his back and floated and

watched puffy cloud ships sailing against the bright blue sky. It was wonderful here, so still and cool in the shallow brook under the arching trees.

Diane and Joel caught up with him and they played water tag, swimming around and around in circles. At last they stopped, panting, and just stood chest deep in the clear water.

"Isn't this great!" exclaimed Diane. "It's our own secret forest swimming pool."

From up on the hill, the sound of a cowbell was heard.

"Lunch!" shouted Joel. "The last one out of the river is a spotted toad."

They came splashing out of the river and dried themselves with towels Joel and Diane had remembered to bring.

"How did the lab work go?" asked Joel.

"Almost finished," said Howie. "Did you know that the log book could be worth a hundred thousand dollars?"

"That's nutty," scoffed Diane. "You can buy one just like it for fifty cents."

"It's not the book, dopey," said her brother. "It's what's in it—all those records and things. That's the evidence Dr. Stevens will use to get his grant to build the research station. Is he really asking the government for a hundred thousand dollars?"

"Just to start," Howie replied, shrugging as if it were nothing.

Diane grinned impishly. "Let me take a look at that log book. I never held that much money in my hand before."

Howie reached down and picked up his shorts from the rock. "Here it is," he said, feeling in his back pocket. Then he stopped short.

"What's the matter?" Joel cried. "You look like a ghost."

Howie gulped. His voice had dried up. "It's . . . it's gone!" he whispered. Frantically he turned his pocket inside out.

"Now, don't get excited," chattered Diane. "It must have fallen out. We'll just retrace your steps."

Howie scrambled all over the small beach but found nothing. "What'll I do? What'll I do?" he cried, wringing his hands.

"Now, wait a minute," said Joel. "Where were you before you went into the river?"

"Oh yes, oh yes," said Howie, babbling with relief. "I was in the bushes hiding from you. That's where it is—it must be."

Howie ran to the bushes and started beating through twigs and leaves. It was remarkable how much alike all the bushes had become. When he had been hiding there, it seemed as if the bush near him was different from all the others. It had fringy leaves. Now, suddenly, there were hundreds of bushes with fringy leaves—and no log book.

Diane and Joel followed him, shoving away at the shrubbery that bordered the beach. Then they combed the beach, looking among the pebbles. Meanwhile the cowbell kept ringing, cheerily calling them to lunch. Clang, clang, clang, it rang right through Howie's head. It sounded to him like the bell of doom.

"Hey, you guys, don't you hear the lunch bell?" called

a voice, and Bud appeared from the woods leading to the hill.

The three children looked at him with stricken faces. "I can't find the log book," mumbled Howie.

"What?" shouted Bud. "What do you mean, you can't find the log book?"

"It was in his back pocket and it fell out," said Joel.

"We've looked all over," despaired Diane.

Bud knocked one fist into the other. "There goes the ball game," he said. He directed angry words at Howie. "Don't you realize that our whole research grant depends on the contents of that book? We don't have any more time to gather evidence, do you hear? The government gave us ten weeks to prove this place before they make up their minds about the industrial offer. If we don't have our material next week to show them, they'll sell the swamp to the factory developers."

As the words came bombarding at him, Howie's eyes grew hot with tears. "I know, I know," he managed to say.

He sank down on a rock and buried his head in his hands. There was a rustle in the bushes and Tom appeared. Bud explained the situation, exclaiming, "What a stupid fool idea that was—giving the log book to a silly kid!"

Tom's mouth tightened and he gave Bud a piercing look. "All right, all right," he said. "Keep your shirt on. The damage has been done. The only thing we can do is to look for it. It couldn't have flown away. Howie, Joel, and Diane, keep looking in the bushes. Bud and I will search the rocks."

The search continued. Numbly and hopelessly,

Howie kept crawling through the bushes. Then suddenly he heard a shout.

"Here it is!" sang out Tom's voice.

Howie leaped to his feet and ran over to Tom as the others crowded round. There, in a muddy crevice under the rock where Howie had thrown his shorts, lay the log book.

Tom reached down into the mud and picked it up. He brushed a spray of soggy swamp grass off the cover Then he opened it up and looked at the pages.

Howie stared in horror. Each page was streaked and blotted with water. The ink came down in tiny runlets, smearing over the precious information. The log book was ruined!

Without a word, he turned and ran. He didn't care where he was going. He just thrashed wildly through the bushes as the twigs and springy branches whipped cruelly against his face and bare legs. At last he reached the center of the island, not too far from the place where Pepper had been caught in the trap.

He flopped down on a rotting log and wearily let the heavy smells and sounds of the forest overwhelm him. It was hot and sticky, even in the shade. Shafts of sunlight poked through the gloom of the leafy roof, pointing at him and his shame. All around him the trees stood as straight and dark as tall black pencils, their branches lifting and whispering in the breezes, seeming to accuse him. Even a family of bluejays, quarreling high up in a tree, sounded as if they were talking about him. "Stupid kid, stupid kid," they kept screaming.

He dug his toes into the flaky brown earth, deep, deep, deep. He wished he could bury himself in the thick forest and never face the world again. He slumped down and sobbed as if he were emptying out his insides.

After a long time he felt a hand touch his arm. He was not surprised, for he knew that sooner or later someone would come to find him. But when he looked up and saw Dr. Stevens, it was almost more than he could bear. He could not look at the kindly scientist who had such faith in him.

Dr. Stevens didn't ask silly questions about why Howie had run away. He knew why. He just put his arm around the boy and pulled him close as if he were a small child. "It's all right. It's all right," he murmured.

"It isn't," sobbed Howie. "I spoiled the log book and ruined everything!"

"Not really," said the doctor. "The writing in the book is a little smeared, but it is still legible. We'll go to town and get another book and copy over the information. Probably do a neater job than the first time. Those notes needed to be pulled together anyway. It'll make it easier for me to explain my findings if the notes are clearer."

Howie inspected the doctor's face carefully to see if he was just fooling. But Dr. Stevens' blue eyes were as calm and peaceful as Round Lake on a summer's day.

For a moment he felt relieved. Then a feeling of hopelessness overwhelmed him. "I'm no good," he said, digging a fingernail into the soft wood of the log. "No one should trust me. I can't even trust myself. I always mess things up. Like the penicillin I spilled. I almost killed my dog. Like forgetting to do my homework. People are always giving me a second chance and then I spoil things again."

Dr. Stevens reached into his pocket and took out his pipe and a book of matches. Lighting the pipe, he leaned back and said, "Howie, just what is your image of what you would like to be?"

"Sir?" said Howie, not understanding.

"I mean, if you could see a picture of yourself as the man you would like to become, what would you see?"

"Oh," Howie replied promptly. "A scientist, like you."

A quirk of a smile flickered at the corners of Dr. Stevens' mouth. "Good," he said. "But that's an occupation, not a man. I mean, what kind of character would you like to have?"

Howie sighed deeply. "I'd like to be dependable!" That was one thing he wasn't. He had been told that enough times.

Dr. Stevens took another puff of the pipe and blew a spiral of smoke up toward the treetops. "Dependable . . . hmmm. So everything you do is aimed at creating a dependable person."

Howie shrugged. "I try," he said. "But it never turns out right."

Dr. Stevens' clear blue eyes looked straight at him. "I've told you how many batches of Stevens' Ointment I spoiled before it came out halfway well. That took ten years. Tell me, how many years have you been working at this dependable business?"

Howie wrinkled his brow. "About five," he said. "Before that I didn't know what it meant." Then he had to smile as he realized that Dr. Stevens was kidding him. But not completely.

"The human personality," said the doctor, "is very much like anything else we try to create. We try for something and we fail, we try again and we fail again. Did you know, some people go for as long as fifty or sixty years without even knowing what kind of person they are trying to make of themselves? And here you are, only twelve, and already you know what you're aiming for. I think that's pretty good."

"You do?" asked Howie, surprised. "Do you think that someday, if I try hard enough, I can be dependable?"

The doctor smiled. "Just keep working at it. That's the important thing. Don't worry if your experiments fail. Start all over again. One of these days you'll wake up and you'll hear everyone say, 'That Howie Blake . . . he's not very handsome, he's not very smart, but he sure is dependable!'"

Howie couldn't help laughing at Dr. Stevens' silliness, but he knew there was a deep comforting truth behind every joking word.

The doctor stood up and pulled the boy up beside him. "March," he said, giving him a smart slap in the rear. "You've got the whole camp in an uproar and no one's had lunch yet."

Quietly, Howie made his way up toward the camp. He felt a little calmer, but he was still not completely satisfied. He knew he could never feel at ease again until he saw the log book completely restored.

10: The Flood

Although the rest of that Saturday at the camp went off
as if nothing had occurred—a happy lunch of hot dogs
and beans and songs and jokes, and then the usual clean-
up chores—Howie thought he sensed a difference in the
way the scientists treated him. There was not so much
of this man-to-man business. It was more man-to-boy
when they spoke to him.

The change disturbed him. Then, when Dr. Stevens
helped put Pepper safely in the center of the raft, he
said nothing about coming the next week. In fact, he
was very quiet. At last Howie could stand it no longer.

"Will you still be here next week?" he asked the doctor.

"Oh, yes," said Dr. Stevens. "We're planning to stay

until a week from Wednesday. I hope you folks can be here Saturday. We can surely use you to help pack our gear."

At that Howie felt a little more lighthearted. Anyhow, he and the twins were still needed. But all during the week he kept turning over in his mind everything that had happened. The more he thought about it, the more he worried that perhaps Dr. Stevens wasn't telling him the truth about the log book. Maybe he had said the information in the book wasn't ruined only to calm him down. The more Howie thought about it, the more convinced he became that the doctor had just made up the story to make him feel better. If he had been in Dr. Stevens' place, Howie reasoned, he would have done the same thing.

The week seemed to drag on endlessly. Fortunately, it was final exam week and Howie had plenty to occupy his mind to shut out his worrying thoughts. One thing he was determined to do: he was not going to let Mr. Frost down too. Every night he studied and reviewed the work until he was sure he knew everything perfectly. When the exams came, he had no trouble with them and he felt he had done well.

But with the last test out of the way Thursday morning, all his doubts came flooding back. It seemed as if he couldn't live until Saturday, when he would find out for sure whether the log book was all right. On the way home from school with Joel he said, "Let's get an early start on Saturday. We can leave before breakfast and eat sandwiches on the raft."

Joel clapped his hand to his head. "Oh, Howie," he

exclaimed, "I was so busy worrying about the math test, I forgot to tell you."

"Tell me what?" asked Howie, alarmed.

"Diane and I can't go with you Saturday. The family is going to my grandmother's for the weekend."

Howie stared at Joel. This was terrible. "Can't go? Joel, you know I can't handle the raft myself."

Joel bit his lip thoughtfully. "Guess you can't."

"This is the last week they'll be there. They need us to help them pack."

"Well, I suppose they'll have to understand. My folks say we have to go to my grandmother's."

Howie had never shared with Joel his worry about the log book. He felt it was a very personal and painful subject. But now he exploded desperately, "Don't you understand? I have to find out if that log book is all right. Maybe Dr. Stevens was just fooling me."

"I don't think so," Joel started to say reassuringly. But then he saw the look on Howie's face. "Okay, come on over to my house. We'll try to get my mother to think of something. She's usually pretty understanding."

Mrs. Matson was full of doubts. "I don't know. It's a long trip, a hundred miles. We only have the two days and you know how much your grandmother looks forward to spending time with you."

"But it's the last week the doctors will be on the island. It's urgent!" her son pleaded.

"Let me call Dad. Maybe he can think of something."

Mrs. Matson went to the telephone and called her husband at his place of business. The boys could hear her saying, "But it means so much to the children."

Howie immediately acquired a new liking for her. She was understanding and she didn't ask a lot of prying questions either.

She came back smiling. "Dad says that if you promise to be back at one o'clock we can still get to Grandma's for dinner. I'll call her and tell her we'll be a little late."

"Oh, thank you," Howie breathed in relief. "We'll start out at dawn and be sure to come back in time."

Saturday turned out to be cloudy. "I'm glad you're coming back early," said Howie's mother. "It looks like rain and I wouldn't want you out on the river in a storm. Don't linger if it starts to rain."

The minute they beached the raft and Bud and Tom came running down the hill to meet them, Howie began to feel better. They seemed to have gotten over their annoyance at him completely. They were full of questions about Pepper's condition and were happy to hear that the dog was beginning to walk around a little.

Dr. Stevens greeted them warmly. He had a twinkle in his eyes, as if he had some surprise at the back of his head. Howie ached to ask him about the log book but he couldn't bring himself to do it.

"We can only stay a little while," Diane explained. "Please tell us how we can help you pack up."

Dr. Stevens shrugged helplessly. "There's so much, I don't know where to begin. I don't know how it happened, but we seem to have twice as much stuff here as we came with. Tom is going to take a load down to the college in the motorboat this afternoon."

Diane went into the sleeping tent and looked with dismay at all the things thrown around. "Just like men," she shook her head. "Can't keep anything in order. How about packing up some blankets? You don't need so many in the warm weather. Then we can gather together some of the extra canned goods." She rummaged in the packing-box cabinet. "Say, you have enough evaporated milk to feed an army!"

Dr. Stevens sighed gratefully. "Every camp needs a woman."

Under Diane's capable direction, the boys filled cartons with blankets and canned goods and took them down to the motorboat. At last Tom came down and put a halt to the operation. "If you put any more junk in there, I'll sink in the middle of the river. Anyhow, Dr. Stevens wants you in the lab tent right away."

As they started up the hill, Howie's heart beat wildly. Now he would know one way or the other whether everything was all right.

Dr. Stevens was waiting for them. "Hurry," he said, "we have an important job to do. I don't like the looks of that sky. We'd better speed things up."

The children and the two student doctors followed him into the tent. Dr. Stevens switched on the light and then he directed the children to stand in a circle.

Very ceremoniously, he handed Howie a book. It looked just like the old log book, but its cover was brand new. Howie glanced through it and his heart leaped with joy. All the information was there, neatly recopied in Dr. Stevens' odd, pointy handwriting.

The doctor glanced briefly at Howie. Then he handed him a pen. "Write," he ordered. "Start a new page."

Dr. Stevens dictated slowly and Howie wrote: "This concludes our study of the area known as the Thorneywoods Swamplands. In our considered opinion, this area would be ideal for a medical research station. The soil abounds in those elements necessary for the study of antibiotic medicines."

Howie was so busy writing, he hardly paid attention to the meaning of the words. He was startled when he heard a loud cheer from Joel and Diane.

"Don't you understand, Howie? This means Dr. Stevens has all the evidence he needs to ask for the grant," said Diane.

"Do you really think the government will give a hundred thousand dollars?" asked Joel.

"Nothing is certain in this world," said Dr. Stevens sagely. "But I think we'll have a pretty good chance."

Suddenly Diane's face clouded over. "It's the end!" she cried. "You're going away and we'll never see you again."

"Not at all," said Dr. Stevens. "I hope we'll be seeing a great deal of one another. If the builders start this fall, the lab should be finished next year. I expect we'll be hiring bright teen-agers as lab assistants. And you have some experience. Think you'd be interested?"

"Oh boy, would we!" exclaimed the three. Howie felt a great burden tumbling from his mind. In spite of everything, Dr. Stevens was still going to trust him with lab work.

Tom had gone over to the radio and was fiddling with it. "Heck," he said, "the radio's conked out. I wanted to get through to the college so they could call Lucy and tell her I'm coming in this afternoon."

"That old set doesn't owe us anything," Dr. Stevens said. "We really don't need it for three days. And I'm

sure Lucy will be glad to see you. Women like sur-
prises."

The light bulb started to swing wildly in a sudden
gust of wind.

"Say, you'd better scoot," Dr. Stevens exclaimed.
"That storm is coming up fast."

Hastily, they ran down to the raft. As Tom climbed
into the motorboat he said, "Let me give you a tow. I
don't trust your paddles in this choppy water."

He tied a rope to the raft and after waving good-by to
Dr. Stevens and Bud, they started off, the motorboat
chugging along and Howie and the twins getting a
bouncy ride on the raft behind. By the time Tom let
them off at the Thorneywoods dock, it had begun to
drizzle.

"Are you sure it's all right for you to go down the
river in a rainstorm?" Diane asked Tom. "Won't you get
all wet?"

Tom laughed. "Don't you worry about me. I'll just
cover myself with one of the blankets if it really comes
down hard. But I don't think the rain will last. You know
these summer showers."

The sound of an automobile horn interrupted them.
They looked up and saw Mr. and Mrs. Matson waiting
impatiently in their car.

"Come on," they called to the twins. "We want to get
started."

Tom waved and started up his motor. The twins
quickly got into the car. Mrs. Matson leaned out the
window and asked Howie if he wanted a lift home.

"It'll take you out of your way," said Howie. "I'll be

all right—I can run fast. I'll be home before the storm breaks."

As he ran the few blocks to his home, the rain started to come down in big fat drops. Little rumbles of thunder came from the hills beyond the dam. Howie was glad to get into the house.

"My, I was worried about you," said his mother. "The water is rough for a little raft."

"Tom gave us a tow with the motorboat," Howie explained.

The sky turned a mottled black and rain started pouring down in torrents.

"Paul," Mrs. Blake shouted up the stairs, "please close the upstairs windows. Howie and I will do the downstairs."

After all the windows had been slammed shut, Paul came down and he and Howie stood at the living-room window looking at the storm. Jagged lightning was tearing through the sky. An angry burst of thunder seemed to explode right over their heads.

Pepper looked up from his bed and whined. From the kitchen they heard their little sister Cindy crying in fear and their mother trying to soothe her.

"Come on, Cindy," called Paul. "Let's play hide and seek."

The game had been started to keep Cindy's mind off the storm, but Paul and Howie soon forgot how grown-up they were. The game became wilder and wilder as the storm rampaged outside. When Paul knocked over a lamp, their mother came rushing in.

"Stop!" she shouted. "I don't know which is worse, the storm outside or the storm inside."

Paul shamefacedly stood the lamp up again. "I guess I just used the energy I was saving for the baseball I was going to play this afternoon. Come on, Howie, let's go down to the basement and press some weights."

Mrs. Blake looked out the window, where the rain was still pouring down as if it were coming from a broken faucet.

"I wish your father would come home," she said. "He said he was only going to stop at the plant for an hour. He had some work to finish up."

"Don't worry," said Paul. "He's probably just waiting for the storm to let up. Come on, Howie."

Howie followed his brother down the stairs. Paul got out his weights and slid fifty pounds on the bar.

He showed Howie how to lift the bar. "Slowly. Now, up above your head."

Howie lifted the weights up beyond his shoulders and up to his ears. "Uh," he grunted. "My arms hurt."

"You've got to practice," advised Paul, making a fist and showing off his arm muscle. "Then you'll get biceps like mine."

Howie couldn't help but admire the bulge on his brother's upper arm, but he scoffed. "Huh. That's not so much. My muscles will be bigger when I'm your age."

He lifted the bar. This time he went a little higher. "Put a heavier weight on it," he puffed.

"No sir," said Paul. "You're only twelve. You'll hurt yourself if you overdo lifting weights. You have to work on it gradually. Now it's my turn."

While Paul was working with the weights, Howie went over to the basement window to see if the rain had let up. The thunder had grown softer and was dying away like a train disappearing in the distance. But the rain was coming down as hard as ever. This was some rain. He had never seen it come down so hard.

A door slammed upstairs. They heard their mother greeting their father, then a loud "No!" from her.

The boys rushed upstairs to see what was the matter.

"Now, don't be alarmed, Mary," Mr. Blake was saying. "This rain will probably end before the dam fills up."

"What happened?" shouted the boys.

"There's something wrong with the floodgates over at the dam. If the rain doesn't stop, the dam is in danger," said Mr. Blake.

Howie's eyes opened wide. "Will we have a flood, Dad?"

"I don't think there's much chance of that," Mr. Blake said soothingly. "This rain will probably end in an hour. But the Civil Defense people have ordered everyone to take precautions. That's why I stayed at the plant so long. We were putting sandbags all around the outside."

The phone rang. Mr. Blake answered. "Hi, Jerry. So you heard about it over the radio. No, I don't think there will be any trouble. How did you folks make out? The sun's out at Chester? Can you imagine! It's still coming down here. Sure, I'll send Paul down to take care of it. Have a good time now. Don't worry."

He put down the receiver. "That was Mr. Matson. They beat out the storm all right, but they heard about the floodgate trouble. Mr. Matson was fixing his hi-fi set in his basement before he left and he's worried about it. Paul, will you go down to their house and take the hi-fi up to the second floor? Mr. Matson said you'd find the back door key under the green flower pot in the garage."

"Green flower pot. Hi-fi set up to second floor. Check," said Paul.

"Make sure Matsons' garage door is closed tightly when you leave," his father instructed Paul as he put on his raincoat and rubbers.

"Right," said Paul, and went sloshing down the hill to the Matsons' house.

The rain kept pouring down like a watery curtain. When Paul came back up the hill he was soaked.

"You should see Merrit Avenue," he exclaimed. "It looks like a river."

"What we need is to get up a petition to put new storm sewers on Merrit Avenue," said Mrs. Blake indignantly. "That puddle is a disgrace." She went over to the window and peered anxiously through the curtains.

"Don't be so nervous, Mary," Mr. Blake said heartily. "It's only an early summer storm. It'll be over soon."

"Who's nervous?" said Mrs. Blake sharply. "Come on, everybody. Let's have dinner."

During dinner everyone talked a great deal. They all seemed to feel that if they talked enough they wouldn't hear the constant drumming of the rain on the roof. The wind had increased and came roaring up the hill. The sound of it whistling through the trees made even the familiar kitchen seem spooky.

Paul went to turn on the radio. Howie noticed his father quickly raise a warning eyebrow and Paul sat down again. Howie understood in an ominous flash that his father was afraid there would be a news report that would upset his mother. Fighting down his own fear, Howie asked for more mashed potatoes to try to distract her attention, even though he really didn't want any.

Mrs. Blake went to the stove to get the potatoes and came fluttering back. She didn't seem like herself at all as she gushed, "Yes, yes, Howie. Have more potatoes. I declare, you'll be seven feet tall if you keep eating so much. When I was a girl I used to go out with a basketball player named Philip. He was six foot seven. He loved potatoes, Philip did."

"He was a potato head, you mean," Mr. Blake teased.

"Now Joe, you didn't even know Philip. That was before I met you."

"I knew Philip, all right. You kept talking about him all the time just to make me jealous."

"Philip finally married Alice Fitzpatrick. They live in Denver, Colorado," Mrs. Blake chattered nervously. The telephone rang and she gave a little shriek, "The telephone!" and dashed to answer it.

Hastily putting down his fork, Mr. Blake followed her. Howie had the feeling his father was expecting this call. He heard his mother say, "It's for you, Joe. It's Frank Page."

"Frank Page is Civil Defense Chairman for Thorneywoods," said Paul. "Wonder what he wants."

The boys, trailed by Cindy, went out to the hall. Their father was saying, "Right. Okay. We'll do that. You informed the neighbors? Fine. Say, how are things out toward Meadowland? My parents live there. Oh, that's good."

Mrs. Blake kept wringing her hands and whispering

loudly, "What's he saying?" Mr. Blake put up a hand for her to be quiet and she stopped whispering.

When Mr. Blake put the phone down he had a frown crease between his eyes. But he spoke with careful calmness.

"Those Civil Defense fellows! They're always looking for some reason to feel important."

"The dam, Joe. Is it going to break?" Mrs. Blake asked urgently.

"Still holding," Mr. Blake replied. "But just to be on the safe side, Civil Defense has assigned certain houses on high ground as shelter stations. Our house is the one for this area. The folks on this block and on Merrit Avenue have been told to come here if there's danger of flooding."

"What about Mama and Papa?" asked Mrs. Blake. "I heard you talking about Meadowland."

"Civil Defense has told the farm families to go to Hillcrest," said Mr. Blake. "The Sachem Motel is putting them up free of charge."

"That's nice of the Sachem," said Mrs. Blake. "Your mother will like that."

"Grandpa too," said Howie. "They have color television at the Sachem."

"My goodness," said Mrs. Blake suddenly. "Do you mean all the neighbors may be coming here? The house is a mess!"

"That's nothing to the mess their houses will be if the dam breaks," said Mr. Blake dryly. "Now, we'll probably be going to a lot of trouble for nothing, but we might as well prepare. Frank suggested that we bring supplies up to the second floor."

An amazing change came over Mrs. Blake once there was something definite to do. All her nervousness seemed to vanish and she started giving orders like a general preparing for battle.

"I have some cardboard cartons in the basement," she said. "Paul, you go down and get them and we'll start packing them with dry cereals and canned goods. We might have to feed a lot of people. Joe, look in the freezer and take out all those chickens I bought on sale this week. I'm going to roast the whole lot right now. I can wrap them in foil and save them to be eaten cold."

The rest of the evening passed quickly as the Blake family labored to bring supplies that might be needed by a dozen neighbors up to the second floor. First of all, there was the food. Then, paper plates and cups and silverware. Next, they brought up all the extra blankets that were stored in the basement.

Every so often someone would go to the window and check on the rain. It still drummed down as if it had forgotten how to stop.

Mr. Blake took Paul aside. "Is your transistor radio working all right?"

"Sure," said Paul. "Why?" He turned it on. The Sparkplugs singing group were wailing, "Why do you make me blue when I'm so in love with you?"

"If it can play on any other station than that teen-age one, turn it to six forty-one. That's the Civil Defense number."

Paul obediently changed the station. An official-sounding voice said, "This is the Thorneywoods Civil Defense. The floodgates at the dam are still jammed. The water is rising, but we do not feel the town is in immediate danger. However, please take supplies up to your upper floors. Fill buckets and bathtubs with fresh water. Conserve all batteries in transistor radios and flashlights. Make sure you have candles handy. If the dam goes, we will have no electricity or fresh water. Some of you have been assigned emergency shelters. If it is necessary for you to go there, you will be so instructed, but do not leave your homes unless you are told to do so. Please keep tuned to this station for further instructions."

"All right, turn it off," said Mr. Blake. "Don't play it unless I tell you to. We don't want the transistors to go dead if we need them."

Paul turned off the radio and put it in his pocket.

"Let's get the fresh water and candles," said his father. "I didn't think of that."

It seemed strange going to bed surrounded by boxes of food and extra blankets. Howie placed Pepper's bed next to his and patted the dog's head.

"Good night, Pepper," he said. "If the dam breaks, I'll take care of you."

He curled up and tried to go to sleep, but the thought of the dam filling up with water made him restless. He tossed and turned. The rain kept drumming down. He noticed that the street light outside his window was awfully bright. He had never thought of that before. At last sleep crept up on him, pushing out thoughts of the dam. He sank deeper into his pillow. He didn't care about floods. He just wanted to sleep.

About an hour later a low rumbling sound broke into Howie's sleep. He opened his eyes and listened uneasily. The rumbling continued, a cracking, sliding sound from far away. Then the street light gave a sudden flash and went out.

Howie blinked his eyes. It was very dark. However, after a few moments he was able to make out the shapes of the furniture and the mound in the next bed that was Paul, still asleep. He groped his way to the window and looked out. The green lights on the parkway were gone. The shapes of the houses across the way looked like black lumps in the rain.

Then there was a wild knocking at the front door. Paul rolled over in bed and groaned sleepily, "What is it?"

"I think the dam's gone." Howie began to shiver.

The knocking continued. Howie could hear his mother and father rush out of their bedroom and down the stairs. Paul got out of bed and the boys followed their parents.

Mr. Blake opened the door and a crowd of people ran in, all talking at once.

The first one in the door was Mrs. King, carrying her poodle, Fifi. She was wearing purple slacks and a polka-dotted red blouse. You could tell she had gotten dressed in a hurry. She put Fifi down and the dog rushed up the stairs to have a barking contest with Pepper.

After Mrs. King came Mr. King and then the Morses with their two sleepy little boys still in pajamas. Then came Mr. and Mrs. Cleary, carrying their baby.

They were carrying suitcases and bundles that were streaked with mud and they spoke in frightened, soft voices. Mrs. Morse had a pair of silver candlesticks in her hand.

"They were my mother's," she sobbed. "I'd die if anything happened to them." ·

Mr. Blake and Paul helped carry the bundles upstairs. Meanwhile Mrs. Blake kept chattering away as if she were giving a party.

"We're all perfectly safe here," she kept saying. "Civil Defense assured us the water would never reach this high."

As they all trooped up the stairs, Howie looked back. He saw a trickle of brownish water coming in under the front door, but he said nothing about it.

The Morse boys were given Paul's bed and Paul wrapped himself in a blanket on the floor. The Cleary baby was tucked into a bureau drawer on the floor in Cindy's room, while the adults gathered in hastily assembled chairs in Mr. and Mrs. Blake's room.

Howie lay tensely under the covers in his own bed, listening in the darkness. He heard the rain against the windows and, from his parents' room, the excited voices of the adults.

His mother was still chattering away. "My, my, isn't this nice," he heard her say cheerily. "We haven't been together like this since the block party last summer."

Howie knew she was talking so much because she was nervous. That made him nervous too. He just lay there, wide-eyed, as the sounds in the next room died away and were replaced by snores. Then, suddenly, he heard a dull boom.

He got out of bed and edged quietly around Paul's bed, where the Morse boys were sleeping with contented little sighs.

Paul raised his head from his blanket. Howie crept under the blanket next to his brother. He started to tremble and Paul put his hand on him, saying, "Don't be scared. The water won't come up here."

"What was that boom?" Howie whispered.

"I don't know. Explosion of some sort." Paul got up on his knees and looked out the window. "Something's burning."

Howie looked out too. Over toward the river a bright orange flare fanned in the darkness.

"Wow!" said Paul.

"Looks like the shoe factory," Howie exclaimed.

"Maybe the boiler burst," Paul guessed. "That sometimes happens in a flood. Too much pressure from the water."

"I hope no one was hurt," said Howie.

"I doubt it. Everyone got out of that part of town long ago."

Suddenly a thought hit Howie. He almost shrieked at Paul before he remembered the Morse children sleeping in the room. "Dr. Stevens and Bud! They're caught in the swamp!"

"Oh, don't worry about them. They probably took their boat and went to Sumner," said Paul.

"They couldn't. Tom took the boat down the river to the college. They don't even have the radio. It was broken and Tom took it with him to be repaired."

"Holy smoke! They're in some spot."

"We've got to help them," Howie cried.

"How are you going to do that in the middle of the night? Swim?" asked Paul.

"Let's try the telephone. That sometimes works even when the electricity is off."

The boys made their way downstairs. When he reached the bottom of the stairs, Paul grabbed Howie's hand. "Watch out," he warned. "It's slippery."

Mud and water had washed in under the front door, coating the floors with slime. The boys walked and slid over to the telephone. Paul reached to turn on a light. Nothing happened.

"Oh, I forgot," he said. "No electricity."

Howie felt around until he found the telephone. He lifted it to his ear but nothing happened. Frantically he jiggled the hook. Still nothing.

"It's no use," said Paul. "The telephone's dead."

They groped their way over to the living-room window. The rain had stopped at last.

"It's almost dawn," said Howie.

Paul stood beside him. Together they watched the blackness draining from the sky and a band of yellow rising in the east, announcing the arrival of the sun. Bit by bit the sky brightened and a strange world came into view.

A lake of still gray water covered the lawns and the street. The water had reached the level of their front porch, making the house seem like a funny-shaped boat. A lone porch chair bobbed on top of the water that covered the front lawn.

As they looked down the hill, they caught their breath. The white peaks of houses and second-story windows seemed to be floating in the water. Howie squinted through the trees to see the Matsons' house. A gold horse weathervane twirled merrily on the peak of their garage roof as the waters lapped just below. Down toward the river a wisp of smoke floated up from where the fire had been. As the sun grew brighter, the boys could see a pile of blackened rubble.

"Good Lord!" exclaimed Paul. "The whole factory collapsed!"

"Do you think Dr. Stevens and Bud are all right?" Howie asked, pressing his nose against the glass as if by doing so he could see clear up the river and into the swamp.

"Sure," said Paul. "You're always telling us how smart Dr. Stevens is. He'll think of some way out. Anyhow, I'll

bet the college has already sent a boat to get them."

Howie pondered. "That's right. The college wouldn't just leave them there."

A wail from upstairs interrupted them.

"That must be the Cleary baby wanting her breakfast," smiled Paul.

When the boys went back upstairs they found the place in a turmoil. Mrs. Cleary had taken a bottle from an insulated bag and was worrying about whether the milk was still all right for the crying baby to drink. Cindy had discovered to her delight that the Morse boys were there and the three small children were racing around playing Indians. Fifi, realizing that Pepper

could not walk, sat in front of his box and barked at him. After a painful attempt to climb out of the box and chase her, Pepper had settled for just barking back.

Meanwhile, Mrs. King and Mrs. Morse stood at the window and gazed at their drowned houses. "Ooh," moaned Mrs. King, "my furniture. My new drapes. My carpets!"

"How's the downstairs?" asked Mrs. Blake as she tried to convert a desk top into a breakfast table.

"Slimy, but usable," replied Paul.

"Howie, count the people so I can know how many bowls I need. It's a good thing I had these paper cups in the closet," said Mrs. Blake, getting out boxes of cold cereal.

As Howie went around counting, he heard an excited voice coming from Paul's transistor radio. Everyone gathered around to listen.

"Jammed floodgates and a break in the dam have caused a flood in the Thorneywoods area. There has been widespread damage, including the destruction of a shoe factory that was demolished when the water pressure caused a boiler in the basement to burst. Fortunately, there was no one in the factory at the time.

"Fears have been expressed for the safety of Dr. Arthur Stevens, prominent physician, and his assistant, Bud Calhoun, who were doing experimental work in the swamplands just north of Thorneywoods. Searchers in the treacherous swamps are hampered by the fact that they do not know exactly where the scientists' camp is. It was hoped that Tom Reynolds, Dr. Stevens' other assistant, could be flown in by helicopter from the James Medical College to direct the searchers. However, Mr.

Reynolds, who traveled from Thorneywoods to the college in an open boat during the storm, is suffering from exposure. Doctors have forbidden him to leave his bed."

"But I know where the camp is!" Howie shouted, as if the man on the radio could hear him. "I can lead the searchers!"

"Take it easy, son," said Mr. Blake gravely. "Our problem is contacting the authorities to let them know that."

"Can't we send out signals like they do on a ship?" begged Howie.

Mr. Blake considered a moment. Then he said, "I know. We'll rig up a flag and hang it from the window."

He tacked a white pillowcase to a broom handle and stuck it out the window. The signal flapped in the breeze.

"That should be visible for quite a distance," he said. "Sooner or later someone will come to investigate."

Howie sat at the window and waited. The noise of the adults and children and dogs continued, but he paid no attention. He just strained his eyes for the sight of someone coming to find out about the white flag.

At last a small boat chugged up the street and grounded on the sidewalk underneath the shallow water. A man in high boots got out. Howie opened the window and yelled "Hey!"

"Anything wrong here?" asked the man. "We saw your signal."

"No," shouted Howie. "But I know where Dr. Stevens and Bud are. Please take me to the search party."

The man looked at Howie in astonishment. "You know how to find Dr. Stevens? How come?"

"I used to go and help him," said Howie impatiently. "Please, I want to help find him."

"You bet!" the man exclaimed. "Come down here and we'll take you right over to the searchers."

Howie started to run for the stairs, but his mother caught hold of him. "No, no!" she cried. "You can't go to the swamp. I won't let you. You heard the man on the radio. It's treacherous!"

Mr. Blake gently took her hand away. "He must go, Mary. Two men's lives are at stake."

Mrs. Blake started to cry. But she wiped her eyes and said, "Let me find your boots."

Together, they went down to the sodden front hall. Mrs. Blake dug Howie's snow boots out from the pile of rubbers in the rubber box. She insisted that he take his raincoat too, although the sun was shining. Then he opened the front door, waved good-by, and sloshed through the water to the waiting boat.

11: Rescue

It was queer to ride in a boat down your own street on a sunny June morning. The water shone under the blue sky like a mirror. Trees rose up in the middle of the new lake, their leaves fluttering like little green banners. There were even birds singing in the branches.

The two-story houses at the bottom of the hill had water up to their second-floor windows. As for the ranch houses, they were practically submerged. Howie pointed out bands of brown mud around the sides of the houses.

"Water's receding," nodded one of the two men in the boat, who had introduced himself as Mr. Kent. "That's the water line where the flood reached."

All sorts of things came floating past. There was a

playpen, trailing a bright red plastic pad. Then came a flower box, upside down. A splintered bamboo rake slid by, then a couple of empty garbage cans. When they passed the shopping center, the parking lot looked like a little sea full of black water.

"The supermarket had bags of peat moss stacked up outside," laughed the other man, whose name was Mr. Conklin. "It's the first time I've ever seen a peat moss lake."

Mr. Kent laughed too, but Howie didn't feel like laughing. He was too worried about Dr. Stevens and Bud.

"I see they have the National Guard out," commented Mr. Conklin, pointing to some soldiers with rifles who were sitting in rowboats in front of the stores. "That's to prevent looting. You never can tell. Someone might take advantage of the situation and try to steal stuff inside the stores."

As they got closer to the river, Howie could hear the thump of giant pumps. The pumps were sucking up water in great gulps and spilling it back into the river. The roadway near the river had been pumped out so it was only ankle-deep in water.

As Howie and the two men got out of the boat and started walking, Mr. Kent explained, "If they can get this road dried up they can set the pumps further inland." He pointed to some men who were uncoiling long black hoses. "The hoses will bring the water to the river."

"That river doesn't need any more water," exclaimed Mr. Conklin. "Will you look at that!"

Howie gazed at the place where the bank of the river

had been. But now there was no bank—the water came all the way up to the road. Sounds of shouting and hammering came from where the big dock and the boathouse had been.

It looked as if a giant hand had come down on the small boats and piers and smashed them into wood splinters. Loose planks were floating out in the river. Army engineers were trying to gather up as much of the wreckage as they could and stack it in a huge pile. Howie thought sadly about his raft. Somewhere out there in the midst of the wreckage must be the shattered pieces of the *Diane*.

Even the large docks across the way in Sumner were full of caved-in places. A big barge lay on its side in the mud. The bridge, which had been closed to traffic, gleamed in the sun high above the wreckage, empty as a ghost bridge.

It seemed very quiet without the tooting of busy river boats. The only things moving were two official-looking gray Coast Guard cutters that had traveled up the river from their base on the ocean. One of them was pulling a barge painted white with a big red cross on its side, piled high with boxes and crates.

"That's good," sighed Mr. Kent. "The Red Cross supply boat has arrived. We'll be needing that food, especially milk for the babies."

Howie thought of the Cleary baby. He had never thought of what would happen to her when the small supply of milk in the house was used up. It was good that the Red Cross had remembered about the babies in the midst of everything.

Army engineers had set up a temporary dock made of

oil drums and planks. Mr. Kent led Howie along the planks to where one of the Coast Guard boats was anchored. Mr. Kent spoke to a ruddy-faced man with gold braid on his hat. At Mr. Kent's words, the man turned to Howie excitedly.

"Mr. Kent tells me you have been to Dr. Stevens' camp. Do you think you could find it again?"

"Oh, yes, sir," said Howie eagerly. "I can find it. I know I can."

The officer, whose name was Captain Kelly, looked Howie over until he began to feel rather small and uncomfortable.

"Are you sure it's all right with your parents for you to go out there?" he asked.

"Yes," Howie answered impatiently. "Please, can we go now?"

The captain signaled to a small motorboat. As the boat came over to the dock, he leaned down and said to two Coastguardmen, "This boy is Howie Blake. He says he can lead you to Dr. Stevens' camp. I think it's worth a try."

The Coastguardmen in front put up a hand to help Howie into the boat. He was very tall and had jet black eyebrows.

"Glad to have you aboard," he said. "My name's Bob Wolf." He waved his hand toward his partner, a wiry young fellow with close-cut curly brown hair. "That's Mike Rocco."

Mike reached over and shook Howie's hand.

Captain Kelly went into the cutter and brought out a Thermos of hot coffee and some blankets. "These are for

Dr. Stevens and his assistant," he said. "Let's pray you get to use them."

Bob and Mike saluted the officer and Bob started the motor. As the boat headed up the river, Mike said soberly, "Howie, we want you to understand that those swamps have been searched over and over since daylight. We may not find your friends. Or we may find them and . . ."

Mike did not finish the sentence, but Howie knew what he meant. There was a very good chance that Dr. Stevens and Bud had been drowned. A lead weight seemed to drop down into the pit of his stomach.

"I know," he said in a low voice.

The motor of the little boat started to whine and the boat pitched and swerved from side to side.

"It's the current," said Bob. "All that water is rushing downriver and we're bucking it."

As they continued upriver, the current became worse. It seemed as if they were traveling sideways rather than forward. Howie gripped the edge of the boat to keep from being pitched overboard.

"There's Round Lake," said Mike. "The fellows who were here this morning said that's the hardest part."

Calm little Round Lake had become a boiling whirlpool. Water was rushing through a crumbled hole in the dam and dashing in fountains of foam into the lake. On the mountain men were laboring to stem the frenzied river by piling a makeshift barrier over the hole in the dam. Other men were working at the dam's sides, trying to repair the floodgates so the water would be diverted into the drainage pipes.

The boat spun crazily in a circle, its motor almost useless. Howie pointed a quivering finger at the stream where the cattails grew, although the cattails were now invisible beneath the water.

"There," he said. "We go into the swamp over there."

Bob tried to veer the boat toward the stream, but the current swept them past the opening. "Take the oars," he panted.

Mike and Howie each took an oar and pushed against the whirling water. Slowly the boat eased over to the side of the lake and slipped into the stream. Although the stream was swollen to twice its normal size, the

water was calm and the going was easier here. The
motor purred and the boat moved along to the entrance
to Deadwood Lake.

At the sight of the lake, Bob and Mike gasped, just as
Howie and the twins had done the first time they saw it.

"This looks like something out of science fiction," Bob
exclaimed.

"It's not," said Howie, a little touchily. "Deadwood
Lake is full of valuable mud, the stuff they can get antibiotic medicines from. Dr. Stevens is going to put a
medical research plant here." He bit his lip. First they
had to find Dr. Stevens.

"Better be careful," he warned as the boat moved into the center of the lake. "There's a lot of stuff drifting around under the water here."

Mike turned off the motor so the whirling propeller wouldn't be caught in the floating debris. He looked inquiringly at Howie. "Where now?"

Howie's eyes searched the borders of the lake looking for the entrance to the little river that led to the camp. Then, to his horror, he realized that all the landmarks were gone. Rising water had covered the original shoreline. Familiar trees had toppled over into the water.

Panic-stricken, he looked about. He felt just as lost as he had on the day he and the twins had drifted aimlessly all around the lake trying to find the way out. They had only found the little river by chance. Once they had learned the landmarks, it had been a simple matter to return to it, but where were the landmarks now?

He felt sweat break out on his forehead. "Over there," he said uncertainly, pointing to a clump of trees that looked familiar.

Bob and Mike rowed the boat over to the trees, gingerly avoiding rotted stumps. They started into a little inlet, but Howie exclaimed in despair, "No, that's not the way."

He could see it was one of the little dead ends that had fooled him and the twins the first time.

Bob and Mike turned around and rowed back to the middle of the lake. They rested their oars and waited sympathetically for Howie to decide what to do.

It was very silent in Deadwood Lake, even quieter than usual. The only sounds were the slither of a school of small fish under the scummy green surface of the water and the buzz of an early insect. The sky, blue and so far away, arched quietly over the ruined forest. Everything, it seemed, was waiting for Howie's next move.

This was no time for wild thinking. He had to reason out the situation and think very carefully. Beneath the heavy silence of the swamp were the echoes of the voices of all the people who had ever said to him, "You never *think*."

Gripping the sides of the boat until the knuckles of his hands were white, Howie reached into the confusion of his mind and tried to remember everything he usually saw when he went to the camp. He recalled a clump of laurel with shiny green leaves at the entrance to the river. His eyes roamed the shores of the lake, pleading for the sight of the laurel, but all he saw was endless water.

Mike's oar slipped in his hand. The splash as the tip hit the water sounded very loud in the silence.

A noise breaking the silence of Deadwood Lake! A vague feeling of something familiar came to him. Then a memory came flooding back . . . here in the lake the first day with the twins . . . they were frightened, especially by the awesome silence of the place.

And then there had been a sound that excited Pepper. A bird, that's what it had been—a big gray catbird flying over from its nest in one of the living trees on the island.

"We must row around and listen for the sound of birds," he told Bob and Mike.

Bob and Mike obeyed without question. There was

something in Howie's manner that made them feel he knew what he was doing. Howie began to feel more sure of himself, too. At least he had a plan.

Rowing as quietly as they could, the three strained their ears to catch the slightest hint of a bird call. But the forlorn trees stood with naked branches empty of birds. No adventurous bird would fly into the swamp seeking insects today. They were all huddled in their nests on the island, probably still frightened by the flood.

Then, suddenly, Howie heard a long, mournful "caw" rising into the air from somewhere in the distance. He held up his hand and the men stopped rowing. Very calmly and deliberately, Howie waited for another bird call. It was not enough to know the general direction from which the sound had come. He had to pinpoint the exact location.

At last he heard, faintly, an answering "caw."

"Over there," he ordered. "Near those two trees close together."

The men rowed over to the two trees. Howie looked at the water near them. A green leaf flickered up from submerged bushes, catching sunlight on its shiny surface.

"Laurel!" he cried. "Keep going. This is the way out of Deadwood Lake."

Bob and Mike steered the boat past the laurel. Gradually trees, their trunks sunk in water, but with green leaves, appeared.

"Look for an old cypress shaped like a triangle," Howie said tensely. "That's where the river branches. We turn to the left to get to the island."

As the cypress, now deep in water, came into view, a feeling of terror came over Howie. He knew they would find the camp without trouble. That was no longer the problem. But what would they find when they got there? Each stroke of the oars made him feel more panicky. He had the greatest desire to tell Mike and Bob to turn the boat around and go back to Thorneywoods.

Bob reached over and laid a hand on Howie's arm. "Have courage, boy," he said.

"I'm all right," said Howie unsteadily. "Just keep on rowing."

"There's the island." Howie pointed. It was hard to tell where the island began and the river ended; all you could see was a clump of trees in the midst of the water.

Mike took a megaphone from the bottom of the boat and handed it to Howie. "Call through this," he said. "Then we'll listen for an answer."

As the boat neared the island Howie noticed what looked like a patch of snow in the water. But as they drew closer he saw it wasn't snow. It was the white canvas of the two tents floating among the trees.

His heart gave a lurch at the sight, but he lifted the megaphone to his lips. "Dr. Stevens, Bud," he shouted. "This is Howie. Please answer. Please tell us where you are."

Some frightened birds came chattering out of a tree.

"You'll have to try again," said Mike. "We can't hear anything over the racket those birds are making."

When the sound of the birds died down, Howie raised the megaphone and called again, "Dr. Stevens, where are you? Yoo hoo, Dr. Stevens."

He put the megaphone down. The three listened.

Then, very faintly, they heard "Yoo hoo," coming from the woods.

It could have been a bird call. Or it could have been a man. Bob and Mike headed the boat into the woods, scraping along through the trees. At one point the boat caught on some bushes hidden under the water. The men pushed with the oars and Howie shoved them free by pulling on a tree trunk.

"Dr. Stevens," Howie called again.

"Yoo hoo," they heard again. This time there was no mistake. It was no bird.

"Over here," said the voice. "In the oak tree."

Howie could not wait for the slow progress of the boat. He scrambled out and half waded, half swam over to the oak tree.

He looked up. There were Dr. Stevens and Bud, looking like huge birds, each sitting in a crotch of the tree.

Something came loose in Howie and he laughed. He laughed and laughed. "What are you trying to be, robins?" he called. It was a funny thing to say, but it just popped out.

"No. Roosters," called Bud. "What took you so long?"

"You forgot to leave a forwarding address," called Mike.

Mike and Bob reached up their hands and caught Bud and Dr. Stevens as they came sliding out of the tree and into the boat.

"I believe I shall spend the rest of my life bent over in the shape of that tree," said Dr. Stevens, painfully sitting down. "Here, Howie, take this." He handed over a familiar black book.

Howie turned the precious logbook over in his hands. It was still dry. The records it contained were safe.

"Couldn't lose the log, you know," said Dr. Stevens. "Didn't want all our research here to go to waste."

Bob took out the blankets and Dr. Stevens and Bud gratefully wrapped them around their sodden clothes. Then Mike poured each of them a cup of hot coffee from the Thermos, which they gulped down eagerly.

"What happened?" asked Bud. "We were sound asleep in our tent when boom, we found ourselves in an ocean."

Howie told about the dam breaking and the flood in Thorneywoods.

When they reached Deadwood Lake Dr. Stevens said in amazement, "How in the world did you ever find your way to the island? Everything's so changed here."

"We listened for the birds," said Howie simply. "That was our clue to where the island was."

Dr. Stevens smiled. "You're quite a boy, Howie. Quite a boy."

As the boat entered Round Lake, they noticed that the wild currents that had tossed them around before had calmed. The dam was shining damply in the sun, but the hole had been stopped up and water was no longer pouring over the top. Instead, it flowed in its usual peaceful manner through the drainage outlets.

"The floodgates are fixed!" Howie cried.

Men were still working on the dam. When they saw the little motorboat chug into the lake with Dr. Stevens and Bud safely aboard, they stopped what they were doing and gave a loud cheer.

"Wonder what they're so excited about," said Dr. Stevens.

At Dr. Stevens' remark, Mike and Bob laughed. "Don't you know the whole country is worrying about you and Bud? The national news services were carrying the story this morning."

Dr. Stevens looked astonished for a moment. Then he gazed at the wreckage of the Thorneywoods piers.

"What a mess!" he exclaimed.

"You should have seen it this morning," Bob commented. "This is good."

Suddenly Howie saw something familiar floating in the midst of the wreckage. At first he couldn't believe his eyes. Then he was sure.

"Hey!" he yelled. "Over there. It's the *Diane!* It's my raft!"

Dr. Stevens peered in the direction in which Howie was pointing. "You're right," he said. "It is the *Diane.*"

"Can you steer the boat over there?" asked Howie excitedly. "I want to get it."

Mike obligingly changed course and went over to the little raft bobbing in the water. Howie reached out and caught hold of it. It was a bit battered but still seaworthy.

"Imagine," he said. "The *Diane* rode out the flood."

"A soundly made craft," said Bob approvingly.

With the raft securely tied behind the boat, they continued down the river to the dock where Captain Kelly had his headquarters. At the sight of Dr. Stevens and Bud, Captain Kelly let out a shout. All the Coastguardmen working nearby ran out on the dock. Many hands were offered to help the men out of the boat.

"We'll get you and your assistant over to the hospital, sir," said Captain Kelly. "You're suffering from exposure."

"Nonsense," said Dr. Stevens. "Never felt better in my life. Just a few kinks in my bones, that's all. Part of that is old age and the rest will be fixed by a little nap."

"You can come to my house," said Howie quickly.

"That would be fine," replied Dr. Stevens. "But first we have to get word to the college and our families that we are safe."

"There's a radio transmitter in the cutter," said Captain Kelly. "I'll get the medical school."

When the medical school was contacted they heard Tom's voice. "Are you all right? Are you all right?" he kept saying in a thickly hoarse voice when he spoke to Dr. Stevens.

"Certainly," said Dr. Stevens. "What about you? You sound as if you have a cold."

Tom sneezed. "Just a small one. I got caught in the rain last night."

"Take care of it," Dr. Stevens advised. "Here, I'll give you Bud."

"Say, Tom," said Bud. "Will you call my mother? Tell her next time I'll listen to her and take my rubbers."

When Howie heard Tom laugh, he felt relieved. Tom couldn't be very sick if he could laugh so loudly.

Newspaper reporters came swarming onto the dock when they heard Dr. Stevens and Bud were there. They were milling about outside the cutter and as soon as they saw them they started calling to them to make a statement or to pose for pictures. When they heard that Howie had directed the rescuers, the reporters surrounded him, too, and started taking his picture. Howie thought it was very exciting, but Dr. Stevens seemed annoyed. Finally Captain Kelly had to hold up a hand saying, "That's enough, boys. Dr. Stevens is very tired."

As the reporters left, one of them waved to Howie and called, "Watch for your picture on the front page, sonny."

"Gee," said Howie, "I wonder what my friends will say when they see me on the front page."

"Poppycock!" snorted Dr. Stevens.

"We've got most of the water pumped out of the town," said Captain Kelly. "The trucks can get through the streets now. I'll get you a ride to the Blakes' house."

The town of Thorneywoods no longer looked like Venice with streets of water, but it was certainly messy. The sides of the houses were smeared with mud from the water, and streets and lawns were coated with a thin layer of mud.

Dr. Stevens looked around, a worried frown on his face. "This is a dangerous situation. A flood like this can bring typhoid."

"Tell me," he said to the driver of the truck, "do you know whether they're giving typhoid shots?"

"Yes, they are," the driver replied. "A health station has been set up at the high school. Everyone has to get a shot. In fact, I'd better take you folks there for yours before you go to the Blakes'."

The high school was swarming with people standing in long lines waiting for their shots. A doctor and two nurses, looking exhausted, were at the heads of the lines, trying to inject everyone.

Dr. Stevens went over to the doctor. "Pardon me," he

said. "My name is Stevens. I'm a physician. Can I be of help?"

The doctor stared at Dr. Stevens, his hypodermic needle still raised in the air. Dr. Stevens was certainly not much to look at, with his muddy, bedraggled clothes.

"Dr. Stevens!" exclaimed the doctor. "You're the scientist who was lost in the swamp! It's certainly wonderful to see you here, sir."

"Yes, yes," said Dr. Stevens briskly. "Do you have another hypo needle? Let me help you with this mob."

"Oh no," said the doctor. "You're in no shape to work now. You have to get some rest."

"I'll rest later," said Dr. Stevens. "It's more important to get the typhoid serum into these people as soon as possible. Let me just clean up."

Dr. Stevens injected Howie and Bud first and then waved them away. "You go home," he said. "I'll be along later."

When the truck drew up in front of the Blake house, the whole family rushed out and Howie's mother embarrassed him by kissing him.

"Where's Dr. Stevens?" asked Mr. Blake.

"He's a doctor," said Bud proudly. "He's working at the health station."

Mr. Blake shook his head. "He's a great man," he said. "He's not too proud to heal a dog. He's not too tired to lend a hand in an emergency."

"Where are all the neighbors?" asked Howie.

"The Red Cross set up cots for them in the school," said Paul. "They'll stay there until they can go back to their own homes."

"Isn't this place a mess," said Mrs. Blake as they came into the house. "Mud all over the floors. I'll never get the furniture clean."

"Yes you will," replied Mr. Blake. "And just think—the insurance company will pay for a new carpet. You always said you weren't happy with the color we have."

Mrs. Blake smiled at his teasing. "Well, thank goodness we have a gas stove. That's working even if the electricity is not." She looked at Bud. "I'm going to make you some nice hot soup. Then you're going to get into a pair of Paul's pajamas and get to sleep."

As they came into the kitchen Mrs. Blake shrieked, "Cindy, what are you doing?"

"Baking a cake," said Cindy happily. She had gathered a supply of mud and was busily dumping it onto the middle of the newly cleaned kitchen floor. As she looked up, her blue eyes shone through a mud-streaked face.

Paul reached down and picked up his little sister. "Cindy thinks the flood was caused expressly so she could make mud pies in the kitchen."

Howie looked around at his family. His mother was bustling about getting the soup ready, Paul was trying to clean up Cindy, and his father was scooping the pile of mud from the floor. They were not perfect, but they certainly loved one another.

"I'll go upstairs and fix Paul's and my beds for Dr. Stevens and Bud," he said.

"Thank you, dear," called his mother. "Bring down some blankets and pillows so you and Paul can sleep in the living room."

Dr. Stevens finally finished giving injections at the high school and came to the Blakes' house. He sank gratefully into Paul's bed and was soon sound asleep, while Bud slumbered in Howie's bed.

Night fell and once more Howie curled up next to his brother, this time on the living-room sofa. Paul fell asleep at once, but the day's events kept racing through Howie's mind.

He got up and went over to the window. The world outside was not frightening, like last night, but it was pitch dark. The only light visible was a single emergency flare used by the men working on the generator at the hydroelectric plant. Starlight made the shapes of the houses seem gloomy. Howie felt a little sad. He missed the cheery streetlight outside the window.

He heard a small, creaking noise. Looking around, he saw a pair of eyes gleaming golden in the dark. It was Pepper, painfully making his way down the stairs.

Howie picked the dog up in his arms. "You shouldn't walk the stairs," he scolded. "You're not all better yet."

With the wriggling dog under his arm, he went back to the window. Thump, thump went Pepper's tail.

"Good dog," said Howie, scratching him behind the ears where he liked it best.

Then, before his eyes, appeared what looked like a wonderland of fireworks—first a necklace of green lights on the parkway beyond the town, and then lights flashing on in the houses and buildings everywhere.

Howie heard a little click behind him. He looked up. There was the empty kitchen, all lit up. He blinked, then he remembered that Paul had absent-mindedly

tried to turn on the lights that night so long ago . . .
why, it was only last night . . . when they came
downstairs during the flood.

He turned off the kitchen light. Then he went back to
the window. The streetlight outside cast its familiar
orange light in his face.

"Everything's fine now," he said, burrowing his face
into the soft black hair on Pepper's neck. "All the lights
are on again in Thorneywoods!"